BEARDANCE

WILL HOBBS

BEARDANCE

ALADDIN PAPERBACKS
New York London Toronto Sydney

Copyright © 1993 by Will Hobbs

ALADDIN PAPERBACKS
An imprint of Simon & Schuster
Children's Publishing Division
1230 Avenue of the Americas
New York, NY 10020

Also available in an Atheneum Books for Young Readers hardcover edition.

Manufactured in the United States of America
8 10 9

The Library of Congress has cataloged the hardcover edition as follows:
Hobbs, Will.
Beardance / Will Hobbs.—1st ed.
p. cm.
Summary: While accompanying an elderly rancher on a trip into the San Juan Mountains, Cloyd, a Ute Indian boy, tries to help two orphaned grizzly cubs survive the winter and, at the same time, completes his spirit mission. Sequel to "Bearstone."
ISBN-13: 978-0-689-31867-2 (hc.)
ISBN-10: 0-689-31867-7 (hc.)
1. Ute Indians—Juvenile Fiction. [1. Ute Indians—Fiction. 2. Indians of North America—Colorado—Fiction. 3. Grizzly bear—Fiction. 4. Bears—Fiction.] I. Title. II. Title: Beardance.
PZ7.H6524Bd 1993
[Fic]—dc20   92-44874
ISBN-13: 978-0-689-87072-9 (Aladdin pbk.)
ISBN-10: 0-689-87072-8 (Aladdin pbk.)
0212 OFF

To my nieces and nephews

Annie, Will, Sarah, Matt, Emily, Dan, Christy, Lindsay, and Clay

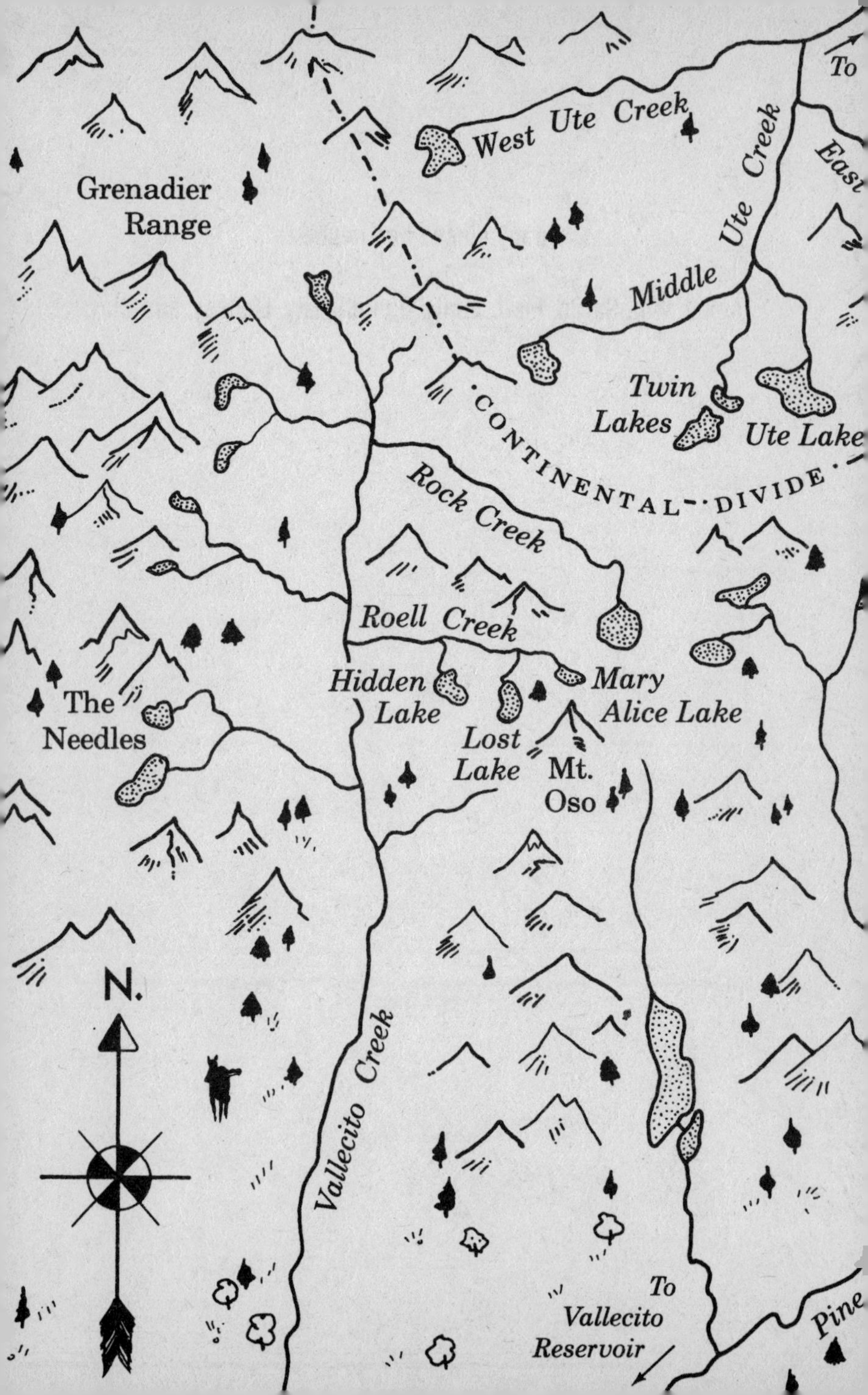

Grenadier Range
West Ute Creek
To
East
Middle Ute Creek
Twin Lakes
Ute Lake
CONTINENTAL DIVIDE
Rock Creek
Roell Creek
Hidden Lake
Lost Lake
Mary Alice Lake
Mt. Oso
The Needles
N.
Vallecito Creek
To Vallecito Reservoir
Pine

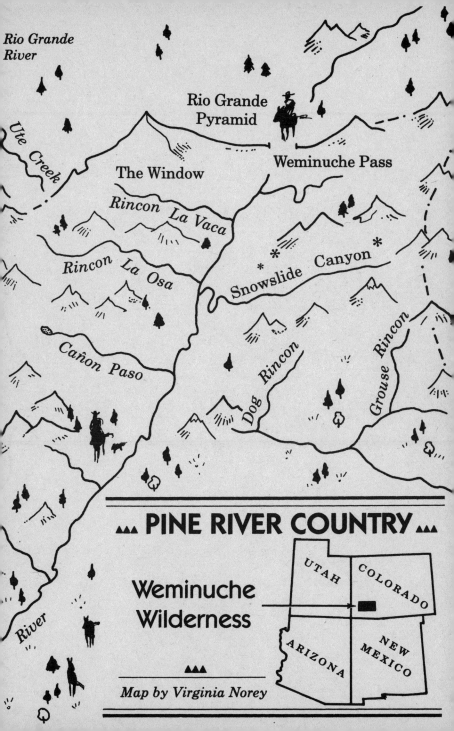

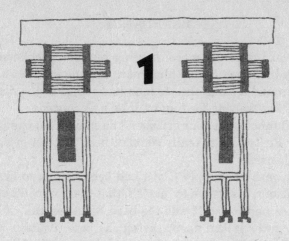

"Do you think there could still be any grizzlies in the mountains?" Cloyd asked.

Up and out of the yellow pines they rode and into the aspens, their quaky leaves shimmering with the slightest breeze. Out of the blue skies and into the clouds and the rolling thunder. Out of the heat and the stale smell of the low country and into the wind-blown freshness of the high.

In search of a lost Spanish gold mine.

Up ahead, the old man stroked the white bristles of his beard and rode on without answering. Cloyd knew that the old man was deep in thought. Walter wouldn't give a quick answer to his question about the grizzlies. Walter knew how important it was.

It was the middle of August, and they were following the Pine River Trail into the mountains. Walter Landis led on the sorrel mare, trailing his four packhorses. Cloyd followed on the blue roan, trailing four more.

Around a bend, the old man had reined in the mare and was waiting for him to draw up alongside.

"Dunno about your grizzlies," he said. "That one you saw Rusty kill, it really could've been the last grizzly in Colorado."

It wasn't the reply Cloyd had been hoping to hear. He'd kept his dream to himself, that there were others. There had to be. It was too hard, knowing that if he had never talked about seeing the bear, Walter's old friend would never have tracked it and killed it. It wasn't something Cloyd could get over. He had boasted to the best hunter, trapper, and tracker in the mountains that he had seen a bear, a huge brown bear.

Cloyd was surprised that Walter had mentioned Rusty's name. Maybe the old man thought enough time had gone by to blur the memory or ease the hurt. For his part, Cloyd was never going to speak the man's name. Words had power, and if he never said the outfitter's name aloud, he wouldn't be giving even an ounce more power to this man who had so much and deserved so little.

The man who killed the bear.

"Of course," Walter continued, "nobody's looked under every tree for grizzes. You've got to figure, there's only one road over these San Juans in a two-hundred-mile swath, and that's Wolf Creek Pass way over above Pagosa. That's a lot of wild country—big enough to have hid that bear for twenty-three years. That's how old the lab in Denver said he was, from the teeth or whatever."

Cloyd regretted that his question had led to talk of the dead bear and the man who killed the bear. He shouldn't have asked his question.

It seemed the bitter taste would never go away.

The red-haired man seemed to have gone away, but hating him, that had never gone away.

Rusty never came anymore to the farm on the Piedra River to check in on his old friend Walter. Cloyd understood why. It was because Cloyd was living at the farm. Cloyd was the only one who knew what really happened up there, high on the Continental Divide.

Rusty would have known that Cloyd wasn't living at the Ute group home in Durango anymore, hadn't returned either to his grandmother over in Utah at White Mesa. He must have heard that Cloyd had stayed at the farm to help the old man get through the winter. But he'd never come by, not even once.

Cloyd still couldn't help feeling that the bear had showed itself to him on purpose. Because Cloyd was a Ute, because Utes and bears were kin. Because Cloyd had found a turquoise bearstone by the burial of one of the Ancient Ones, and had named himself Lone Bear.

There wasn't a day that had gone by that the grizzly hadn't come to mind, almost always as Cloyd had first seen him: standing at the edge of the meadow in the Rincon La Osa with the dark spruce timber behind, and big as a haystack. The bear was standing on two legs, flat on his feet the way people stand, forepaws at his sides, with those enormous claws. The brown bear was just watching him, squinting for a better look, his head swaying slightly back and forth, his forehead wide and dished out a little in the middle.

More than anything, the bear was curious. Alert and intelligent and curious. That's the way Cloyd liked to remember him.

But sometimes that other scene came to mind, the one burned into his memory forever. Time and again it would return without his bidding. On one of the terraces above Ute Lake, the bear was turning over rocks along a line of brush as the red-haired man nocked his arrow and bent his bow. It was a moment that would never let go of Cloyd. He was hollering with all his might into the wind, and the wind was blowing his warning behind him, up and over the Continental Divide. The bear never heard his warning.

Up ahead, Walter was riding out of the trees, and now Cloyd also rode out into the light and the greenness of the longest meadow on the lower river. Here the Pine ran smooth over gravel beds of ground granite, and on the outside of the turns there were deep pools where the biggest cutthroat trout could be found. Cloyd paused for a moment as bits of color in the bushes lining the banks caught his eye. "Walter," he called, "hold up."

They tied their horses at the edge of the trees and then they fell upon the raspberry and currant bushes like bears filling their bellies against winter. The berries were juicy and sweet. The boy and the old man were laughing at the sight of the stain all around their mouths, while their fingers kept working as fast as they could go. "Can't recall berries this prime," Walter observed when his stomach was full. "Must be all the rain."

Cloyd's fingers were still flying. He had a bigger

stomach to fill, and nothing they'd brought along to eat could compare with this.

Walter's old eyes had noticed something up the valley. Cloyd looked and saw a string of horses entering the meadow. Behind, toward the peaks, the tall clouds were beginning to turn dark, and thunder was rumbling. Down on this meadow, though, the sun was still shining. He'd be comfortable in his T-shirt awhile.

Cloyd turned back to his berry picking as the old man kept his eyes on the trail, and when Cloyd looked again several minutes later he saw that the packstring was led by a single rider, a big man with a large face framed by a full red beard and red hair spilling from under a dark felt Stetson. A rifle was scabbarded under one leg. Cloyd's hands stopped their work, and his dark eyes locked on the face almost coming into focus down the trail.

"Could it be?" the old man wondered aloud.

Cloyd was wondering the same thing, and he was hoping the old man was mistaken. The red-haired man had never had a beard before.

The horseman rode closer and closer, close enough that recognition showed in the old man's face. Walter was smiling and shaking his head, surprised to see his old friend looking so different, pleased to be seeing him after so long even if there was reason not to be pleased. "Speak of the devil," the old man said in greeting. He said it in such a way that it was friendly and it wasn't, both at the same time.

Rusty's eyes were on Cloyd, not on his old friend Walter. He nodded to Cloyd, and then he broke out in a big smile all surrounded by the deep red of his beard and mustache.

"Long time . . ." Rusty said in that unmistakable gravelly voice, as he lifted his hat and ran his hand through his wavy hair. "You're the last two people I expected to run into on this trail."

The old man played dumb. "Now why's that?"

The red-haired man's eyes ran to the picks and shovels sticking out of the gear. He was shaking his head and grinning. "Walter, don't I recall you blowing yourself up last summer? Don't tell me you're going to have another go at the Pride of the West!"

"Just out for a ride," Walter replied with a glint in his eye. "Never know when you might have to dig a hole in the ground."

"So what's the long gizmo all wrapped in black on top of that third horse?"

"Broom," the old man quickly replied, with his tongue in his cheek. "We keep a tidy camp."

"Got to be gold you're after," the outfitter said confidently. With another glance at Cloyd, he said, "Sorry I never came by the farm. No excuses, I guess. Glad I saw you two, though—I'm leaving for Alaska real soon."

The red-haired man tied his horses, and then he came back and sat on the edge of the stream bank with the old man. Cloyd stayed well out of the reach of Rusty's crushing handshake and kept to his berry picking. He could stay near, close enough to hear. The red-haired man kept glancing his way, but he seemed to know not to try to speak to him. Walter would know why. There was something between Cloyd and Rusty, and it was because of the lie. The bear hadn't attacked the big man, as Rusty had told the game wardens and the newspapers. Rusty was the one who had surprised the bear, and he'd known it was a grizzly he was tracking.

Cloyd knew now—he'd known for a long time—that he should have told what he saw. He should have told how the bear really died. This man would have lost his outfitting license, would have had to pay a huge fine, and maybe would have even gone to jail for killing an animal that was endangered. But no one else had been there. It would have been his word against Rusty's. Would they have believed him, an Indian kid from Utah who didn't have a father or a mother? Now he would never know if they would have believed him or not.

It had been a mistake to leave it up to the red-haired man to tell the truth. People knew only the lie, and people believed the worst of the bear. No one would ever know what really happened.

Rusty liked to stroke his new beard, long and shaggy like a mountain man's. Cloyd hated him for his vanity.

"So you're leaving for Alaska," the old man was saying.

"You know how much I like it up there. . . . The way I feel, Colorado's just not big enough for me anymore. I might even stay up there one of these times."

As he looked from Walter to Cloyd and back, the red-haired man had a curious expression on his face. "You really haven't heard what I've been doing all summer up in the mountains, have you? Or what I saw back in May?"

Matter-of-factly, the old man replied, "Sure haven't."

The red-haired man seemed a little surprised. "The game wardens and the forest service have been keeping a pretty tight lid on it, but there was one short article in the Durango paper—thought you might have seen it."

"Don't always get the paper," Walter said.

With a quick glance at Cloyd, who for a moment met the man's blue eyes before looking away, Rusty said, "I found a grizzly and three cubs back in May, up in the Rincon La Vaca."

Cloyd felt the breath go out of him, and his throat went tight, and he couldn't breathe. Was it true? Or was it another lie?

The wind was starting to blow. Cloyd realized that the sun hadn't been shining for some time, and he was cold. But he wouldn't go to his saddlebags for his jacket, not now.

"I spent three weeks looking in May," Rusty was saying. "On snowshoes mostly. The animals aren't used to seeing people up there in May—I thought it would give me an advantage. I knew, if there were any grizzlies still around, they had to be uncommon wary even for grizzlies."

The old man's eyebrows were arched high. "Get any pictures?"

"The camera was in my pack at the time. I never had a chance to take a picture. But I know grizzlies, and I know what I saw. The sow was a silvertip, and the cubs were brown, gray-black, and one sort of cocoa-colored. Chances are they were sired by that male I killed last summer. . . ."

The old man turned and addressed Cloyd. "There's your answer, Cloyd. There's not only one grizzly left in Colorado, there's at least four."

With the red-haired man's sharp eyes waiting for his response, Cloyd shrugged and said nothing. His shrug said, Why should I believe you?

It pained the trophy hunter not to be believed by a

kid, an Indian kid, and it showed. He went back to talking to the old man, and now all three were keeping an eye on the weather, which was building fast. "So this summer that's just about all I've been doing," Rusty was saying. "Trying for another glimpse of that grizzly and her cubs. The U.S. Fish and Wildlife Service is all excited. They want proof, and they've had teams of government people and all sorts of grizzly experts combing the mountains this summer. With not a bit of luck. That grizzly's keeping herself and her cubs well hidden."

Up the valley, the rain was already falling. The old man stood up to go to his horse, and then the red-haired man stood up too. "Keep your eye out for those grizzlies when you're up there," he said. "Walter, I guess Cloyd's lost his voice completely over the winter . . . it's a shame. Just in case he's deaf too, tell him I heard how he kept your place open all winter, how he put up two haycrops this summer. I may not have come around, but I've been trying to keep in touch after a fashion."

Walter grinned and said, "I'll tell him."

"How old is he this summer?"

"Fourteen or fifteen—no records."

"Tell him he's looking lean and mean—lost his baby fat, I guess."

Cloyd grinned a little too, despite himself.

"One more thing," the red-haired man said over his shoulder. "Tell him I didn't kill the last grizzly in Colorado after all."

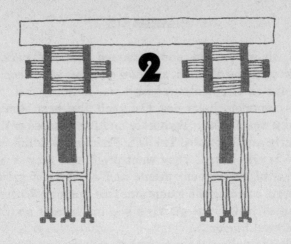

They were climbing, climbing all the time. Cloyd could feel Blueboy's excitement beneath him. Blueboy was a smart one, and he remembered this trail by heart. It seemed the horses knew they were heading tonight for the tall grass in the meadows of the Pine, a horse heaven above these plunging mountainsides, this cascading whitewater.

Grizzlies in the mountains! A mother and three cubs! Maybe Rusty hadn't lied this time, Cloyd thought. Walter Landis didn't think so. The old man said that Rusty had a "monkey" to get off his back. Cloyd didn't exactly know what that meant, but he understood the sense of it. Walter was saying that maybe Rusty had spent those three weeks in May looking for grizzlies because he was having a hard time living with his lie. Maybe he was even ashamed of what he'd done. Maybe.

BEARDANCE

Lightning cracked and its thunder came rumbling through the narrow canyon of the Pine. Rain was bouncing off Walter's ancient cowboy hat, the brown felt one he favored. The Cachefinder was wrapped up good and dry atop one of the pack boxes. The old man's high-tech metal detector had to be kept a secret.

Walter was like that about gold. But at least, over the winter, he'd accepted that his days of drilling and blasting and mucking were finished. As the old man had healed up from his injuries, Cloyd had seen him pick up his beloved *Mining Gazette* less and less. Instead, in the long winter evenings, Walter would pore over and over the stories in a dusty book he'd taken from the very bottom of the parlor's bookshelves. It was called *Lost Mines and Treasures of the San Juan Mountains of Colorado.*

Walter would read the stories aloud, and sometimes Cloyd took a turn. There was one tale in particular they'd come back to two, three times. It was called *"La Mina Perdida de la Ventana"*—"The Lost Mine of the Window."

It was a good story, Cloyd had thought, but the best part was that the lost mine was supposed to be close to the Window, that spectacular notch in the Continental Divide on the high ridge that stuck out from the Rio Grande Pyramid. He could almost believe that a fortune in lost gold was waiting to be found there. It was that kind of place, full of power and beauty, danger and magic.

Still, Cloyd didn't believe in those gold stories. It tickled him, though, how the old man believed every word.

The lost mine had made only a story to think about

until the second cutting of hay was in the barn, and that's when the old man had started talking about the mountains, about going back again. Cloyd was surprised. All summer he'd daydreamed about the high country, but he never shared his daydreams with the old man, who would never again be able to work his mine back in the mountains. For the rest of his days, Walter would carry a bad limp in that right leg that had been so badly broken.

With less than a month remaining until school started up, Walter had come to him, and he had a faraway look in his eyes. "Mostly I just want to see those mountains up close, one more time, while I can still ride. I've never seen the Window, Cloyd, like you have. I want you to show it to me. I want us to see it together."

Cloyd had shaken his head, almost like he was being asked permission; and in a way, he was.

"One more time while I can still ride."

Cloyd was startled. "You've been on a horse again?"

"While you were bucking the second cutting up into the barn," the old man replied sheepishly. "Who knows, Cloyd, we might even find the Lost Mine of the Window. Now wouldn't that be something."

Then the old man confessed that he'd already sent away for "the best metal detector money can buy."

According to the story in the book, the Spanish were supposed to have left three caches of high-grade gold ore behind, two hundred and fifty years before. The old man was sure he was going to find at least one with the Cachefinder he'd seen advertised in his *Mining Gazette*. The Cachefinder was supposed to be brand-new and far better than any metal detector ever made. At least he wasn't going to try to blast open his old gold mine, Cloyd thought.

Cloyd rode up the Pine River Trail grinning about this old man who was always sure that tomorrow would bring greater things than today and who always dreamed his dreams on a grand scale.

Lightning snapped closer this time, and Cloyd snugged his red baseball cap down. Walter had found a good little bench off the side of the trail with a tight cluster of spruces that would shelter them until the storm center moved past.

"It's really steep through here," Cloyd observed as they shared a candy bar.

"Narrow too," Walter replied. "This has to be like that hill country in West Virginia where my father grew up."

"Pretty narrow back there?" Cloyd asked, because he knew the old man would expect him to ask.

The hint of a smile played on Walter's weathered features. "Never seen it myself, you understand. I was born and bred on the Pine before I made my big move to the next stream over, the Piedra. According to my father, that West Virginia country was so steep, all a fellow had to do to bring in his apples was to give the trees in his backyard a shake, an' the fruit would run right down into his cellar."

"That's pretty steep," Cloyd agreed, keeping his face blank as any poker player's.

"So steep they developed a breed of cattle with legs shorter on one side for easier grazing. Even the cornfields were steep. They planted corn by firing the seed out of a gun into the opposite hillside."

Cloyd was trying as hard as he could to keep from smiling. "Did you believe him?"

The old man's ears were turning a little red, and the veins in his forehead and temples were standing up high. "Why, of course I believed him," Walter protested. "I asked my dad once how come his teeth were worn down so bad, like an old horse's. He explained that level ground was so scarce back where he grew up, chimneys crowded the hillsides and gravel was always falling into the pot of beans set to cook in the fireplace. We think *we've* got steep and narrow in our mountains. . . . Back there the dogs had to wag their tails up and down, and you'd have to lie down and look straight up to see the sky."

Cloyd glanced away, stifling his laughter. He wanted to make the old man laugh first. For his part, Walter was trying hard to keep a straight face. It was easy to see that the old man wasn't going to last long. "Is that true?" Cloyd insisted.

"Yes sir," Walter mused. "It was so narrow back there, the moonshine had to be wheelbarrowed out every morning, and daylight wheelbarrowed in."

Now it was raining hard. The horses' rumps and the tarps over their loads were streaming wet. "Did it rain a lot?"

"Why, no," Walter said quickly. "The way I remember hearing it, that was a country so dry, if a drop of water were to hit a man, they had to throw a couple buckets of dirt on his face to bring him to. . . ."

Cloyd couldn't help it anymore and started laughing. Then the old man was laughing too, and his face above his thick white whiskers was all red, and his ears were turning red.

The storm passed, and the horses climbed once more.

Finally Cloyd saw the first of the Pine's upper meadows, miles of meadow green and wide and long, with the spruce-covered mountainsides standing back at a distance. And there was the river, winding its way toward them in gentle oxbows.

" 'He maketh me to lie down in green pastures,' " the old man said reverently.

Cloyd said nothing, only gave Blueboy a pat on his withers and ran his eyes up the valley, up the dark slopes studded with massive granite outcrops. The last creek on the left, another nine or ten miles up the valley and immediately under the Pyramid—that's where Rusty had seen the grizzly and cubs, if indeed he had.

It was important to Cloyd to see those grizzlies, even if it was just as unlikely as finding Spanish treasure. He'd found everything in the school library on grizzlies. He remembered that a grizzly would cover thirty, fifty, even a hundred square miles in its territory. At least Spanish gold didn't move around every day.

Still, he might have some luck left, some bear luck. More than anything, he wanted to see those grizzlies for himself.

"Fresh fish tonight," Walter said. "Fried in cornmeal blankets. If my Ute guide can still produce, that is."

"I can produce," Cloyd assured him. "I've even got flies and lures, and I can always dig worms."

Cloyd came back into camp with six orange-jawed, orange-bellied cutthroats on his willow stringer. The old man had the old sheepherder tent set up and was limping around the fire. "Let's stay a couple of days," Walter suggested. "It'd be a good idea for me to get used to the altitude before we go on up high."

"Gonna try out your metal detector?" Cloyd asked.

15

"Do you walk to school or carry your lunch?" the old man replied mysteriously. "Wouldn't think of it, Cloyd, not with hikers around. Let's keep the Cachefinder hid away in its case. There's no percentage in advertising what we're really up to. When it comes to gold, people get . . . peculiar."

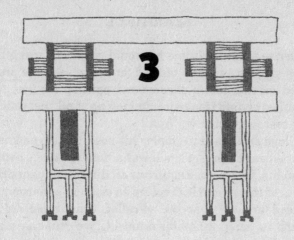

3

The old man understood Cloyd's need to roam in search of those bears. A glimpse would satisfy him, just a glimpse to verify Rusty's words. With only his daypack on his back, Cloyd roamed away from the trail, into the deep woods, across the rockslides, up the grassy avalanche chutes, and into a high basin that had no name on the map.

A little higher, Cloyd thought, and he might be able to glimpse the Rio Grande Pyramid. But he'd spent the day climbing, and now it was time to start down. Heading back for that old man always made him feel good, whether it was on the long bus ride home from school in Durango or charging down off a mountain.

The second day of Walter's rest-up on the Pine, Cloyd said good-bye and set out more deliberately. Again he would leave the trail and go places that hikers would never see, but this time he would go slowly, using his eyes and his ears and his feel for the unseen. He practiced moving like a shadow and pausing for five, ten minutes behind trees without moving at all, just watching and listening.

Cloyd even tried to employ his nose, though he knew that a bear's sense of smell was a hundred times better than his. He watched squirrels caching seeds under the roots of the trees. He crept up so close on a marmot in a boulder field that the so-called whistle pig didn't sound its screeching alarm until Cloyd could have almost yanked the big rodent's tail.

In the afternoon he stayed in one place and watched a shallow pond in a clearing in the trees five hundred or so feet below the tree line. Someone might come to drink at this pond, he thought. Deer or elk or maybe even bears.

His hands found themselves whittling on a piece of spruce. He made a stick that was about a foot long, straight and smooth. It reminded him of the rubbing stick the singers had used at the Bear Dance he had gone to in May at the Southern Ute Reservation down in Ignacio, only thirty miles south and west of the old man's farm.

Cloyd looked around for material to make the second stick, the notched one. The singers had used axe handles, long and hard and perfect for holding deep notches.

By the pond grew a cluster of chokecherry bushes. They would be perfect, if he could find a dead limb. In his favorite class at school, Living in the Southwest, Mr. Pendleton had said that the Utes used to make their bows out of juniper or especially chokecherry. No juniper grew this high, but here was chokecherry. If it would make a good bow, why not growler sticks?

Two bull elk with wide, branching antlers, all in velvet, came out of the woods and approached the pond before their eyes caught the motion he was making. Cloyd never saw them, he was so intent on his whittling. The chips were flying, and a growler stick was taking form.

When Cloyd tried the smooth stick across the notched growler, he was satisfied with the sound. He wasn't worried about scaring off any bears that might be close. Maybe this rasping would attract them! It was this thunder, this scratching and growling of bears, that called to the bears in the mountains all the way from the brush corral at the Bear Dance in Ignacio. This sound called them out of their big sleep with the first spring thunder into a world that was coming to life again for bears and people—kin to each other, as his grandmother often said.

In the earliest times, his grandmother had said, a person could become an animal if he wanted to and an animal could become a person. His grandmother had told him that when he was little, and it had stuck in his mind. As he grew older he realized it was only a story, even if his grandmother didn't think of it as a story. But it was a story he'd always wanted to be true.

When the first people and the animals crossed back and forth, his grandmother said, it made no difference whether they started out as person or animal. Everyone spoke the same language. Back then, words were magical. A word spoken by accident could result in strange consequences. Thoughts spoken could come to life, and what people wished to happen could happen—all you

19

had to do was say the words. Nobody could explain why this was the way it was, his grandmother said. That's the way it was in the earliest times.

When he was little, these stories had been just as real for him as they were for his grandmother. They were still good stories, he thought.

Cloyd kept up the rhythm, the rasping, scratching, growling rhythm of the smooth stick over the growler. It was too bad he lacked the big drum dug into the earth. Eight men rasping over that long, metal-covered drum could create a powerful thunder that ran through the earth. He could remember it coming up through his feet and running through his spine.

The more Cloyd rasped, the more it took him back to May and the Bear Dance. When Walter dropped him off in Ignacio that Friday morning at the Bear Dance and he saw the brush corral, ten feet high and a hundred feet across with the one opening to the east, he realized he'd seen it before. Once, when he was little, his grandmother had taken him from White Mesa in Utah all the way to Ignacio, Colorado, for the Bear Dance. That was back when she used to call him "honey paws" or "short tail." She had told him that the brush corral was round like the inside of a bear den is round.

That first day of the dance had also been the last day of school. At school, Mr. Pendleton was going to show everybody how to make fire with a bow drill. Everyone had failed the day before, with their own homemade bow drills, including Cloyd. One kid had said, "Cloyd can't even do it and he's an Indian."

Cloyd had wanted to go back for the last day and learn the secret of the bow drill. But even more, he didn't want to miss any of the Bear Dance. He'd been looking forward to it all winter, for himself and for the bear who had been killed.

By the pond in the forest, high above the Pine River in the back country of the Weminuche Wilderness, Cloyd began to dance the bear dance as the clouds darkened above him and thunder began to reverberate among the peaks. Three steps forward, three steps back—like a bear dancing to a scratching-tree—as he kept up the rasping of his growler sticks. His dancing took him back to that first day of the Bear Dance, and the thunder took him back to the second, to the unforgettable thunder of that May night with eight men working over that long resonating drum.

He remembered that there had been a storm blowing in that last night of the Bear Dance. It was well after midnight. The storm was close, with lightning displaying in wide, intricate webs and thunder rumbling. The last dance was about to begin, the endurance dance. The Cat Man was advising people to have someone ready to relieve them. Cloyd didn't think he would. There was no way he was going to quit now that the Bear Dance was almost over. He had almost made it, almost danced the whole thing.

He remembered that he was so tired, he didn't feel connected to his feet anymore. He hadn't eaten anything since the dance had started Friday morning. His grandmother had told him once, that was the way they did it in the old days. No eating until the feast, until the Bear Dance was all over.

Keep going, he'd told himself. Keep dancing. Three springing steps forward, three back. The singers were chanting and he felt their growler sticks reverberating up and down his spine, speaking thunder and the scratching and growling of bears. He was exhausted, utterly exhausted. Yet he kept dancing without even knowing that he was dancing.

What happened next he'd never recalled before this moment by this pond. Now that time came back so vividly, his exhaustion seemed to return full force, and he was at the Bear Dance again. This memory had lain deep in his mind, as if at the bottom of a lake. *While his body was dancing, his spirit was rising above.* That's what it was, that's what had happened.

It was an odd sensation, rising up into the air, but not unpleasant. He didn't fight it, but let his spirit drift up, up, until he was high above the Bear Dance, looking down at the wide brush corral and all the dancers and the singers working their growler sticks over the long resonator. Through spirit eyes he looked down at the fire at the center of the dance, the sparks flying into the night, himself in the line of male dancers. And all around, panels of lightning were lighting up the purple clouds.

He could see one of the dancers pawing the air as he danced, just like a standing bear. He could see the woman across from that dancer, in surprise, losing the beat for a moment, and pausing before she continued.

That dancer so much like a bear, he realized from high above, was himself.

Suddenly he was back in his body and in the line of male dancers again. His legs kept moving despite their weariness, three steps forward, three steps back. His hands were pawing the air; he heard himself woof with a bear's voice. Still his legs had that spring in them. He'd danced so long and so hard, he'd danced himself deep into the mountains. He had the sensation that he was moving on four legs. When he looked around behind him, he noticed his tracks, and they were bear tracks!

Cloyd shook himself out of his dreaming and stood up. Shade was overtaking the pond, and it was time to go. It had amazed him, what he'd remembered from the Bear Dance that he had never remembered before. He knew what his grandmother would have said about what happened there. She'd always said that everyone has a "traveling soul" that could leave the body and travel in the spirit world.

He'd always thought that such things could never happen again, that they only happened a long time ago to the old Indians who were all dead now. The spirit world his grandmother had always talked about—he had never really believed in it, at least for him. Only the old people could really believe in spirit people and spirit bears who lived in a spirit world.

But now he knew that for a brief time, he had traveled in the spirit world. And now he wondered if the spirit world was the world of that earliest time his grandmother had talked about, when there was no difference between the people and the animals and they could cross back and forth. Could it have been possible, that he'd really been in the spirit world when he'd looked over his shoulder and seen only bear tracks?

He missed the bearstone. When he'd had the turquoise grizzly in his pocket, he'd felt like one of the old Utes.

It was time to be heading back to the old man, to the camp on the Pine. The bearstone was back at the farm on Walter's nightstand. It had been a good thing to do when he'd given the bearstone away to the old man. Walter got his strength back then, after the terrible accident at the mine. It was the best gift Cloyd had ever given.

"Live in a good way," his grandmother liked to say. "Give something back."

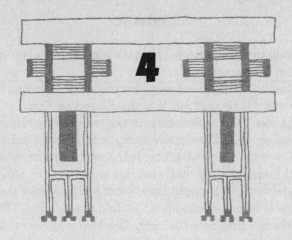

In a few days the horses were rested, and so were the
boy and the old man. They proceeded up the meadows
of the Pine, separated every mile or two by hills
to climb where the trees reached the river and the
whitewater cascaded from one meadow down to the
next.

Cloyd was in the lead when they came to the spot
where Snowslide Creek flowed in from the northeast.
He reined in Blueboy and asked over his shoulder, "You
want to go up to the mine, just to see it?"

The old man ran his hand through the bristles of his
beard. He was thinking about it one way, and then the
other. "I don't think so, Cloyd. The Pride of the West
is a closed chapter. Point me toward *la Mina Perdida
de la Ventana*. I've grown fond of the idea of just col-

lecting that high-grade ore that's already been brought out of the mountain."

Cloyd steered them west up the next drainage, up the steep trail that led into the Rincon La Osa.

At last they broke out into the meadow he remembered so well. They made camp, and then he led the old man to the spot along the Rincon stream where he'd fished the big cutthroat out with his bare hands. All winter he'd thought about what had happened next. "This is where it happened," he told the old man. "This is where I first saw the bear. The bear was over there at the edge of the trees, standing up and sort of squinting at me."

Walter Landis took off his hat and scratched his head, and then he settled himself down on the remains of a spruce, bleached for years by the sun, that had almost been reclaimed by the meadow. "You can't unscramble eggs," the old man said softly. "There's three things that return never: the spoken word, the sped arrow, the past life."

Walter picked a shoot of grass from a clump growing out of the log and began to chew on it. The words he'd spoken seemed for both of them to hang in the air and take shape and power, perhaps more than he had intended.

Return never, Cloyd thought, and he could see the arrow flying off Rusty's bow.

He hated feeling sorry for himself. It reminded him of that year in the group home in Durango when he was angry all the time, when he failed all his classes on purpose, when he bullied kids out of dimes and quarters.

He used to be like that.

He used to be like that before he found the bearstone in the cave high above the old man's farm, before he dreamed of visiting the wilderness named after his own band of Utes. Before he'd worked for Walter, and before Walter had taken him into the mountains.

The loneliness and anger was still inside him, like a poisonous desert plant waiting for a big rain. He could keep it from growing if he didn't feed it. Taking care of the old man and the farm hadn't left any time for feeling sorry for himself. He'd driven the tractor in winter and summer, plowed snow and cut hay. He'd hand-shoveled the deep snow from the walks around the old farmhouse. Every day in winter, he'd taken the axe and chopped the ice to keep the hole in the pond open for Blueboy and the other horses to drink. He'd brought in the firewood all winter and irrigated the fields in the summer and done a hundred other chores. It was a good feeling, to work that hard for someone you cared about.

And here he was, back in the Rincon La Osa, the Corner of the Bear.

Blueboy had grazed close and wasn't ten feet away. The blue roan never strayed far. With his eye on Cloyd he ripped a clump of grass free, then raised his head and began to draw the long shoots across his molars, grinding noisily. The old man had chewed up his own piece of grass, just like a horse.

They heard the sound of horseshoes on stone and looked up to see a rider approaching with six pack-horses behind.

Cloyd recognized the young man who'd come twice

to the farm this summer to buy hay. It was Tony Archuleta, who was always joking, with the flashing smile and the thick black mustache, his hair black as Cloyd's and nearly as long. Cloyd remembered how much Tony Archuleta's eyes had approved of the hay, but Tony had never said it was good hay until he was done bargaining. Cloyd had handled all the sales of the hay; the old man had wanted him to learn. Cloyd knew he'd done well when the man had said in his English that sounded like Spanish, "You're an old coyote."

Tony looked good riding down the Rincon La Osa on his buckskin horse, with his beaten felt hat and his denim jacket and the ancient leather chaps on his legs. His face was dark, at least half as dark as a Ute's. "Walter Landis," the young man sang out, "and his Yuta coyote!"

Cloyd liked that, being called a Ute coyote.

Frustrated at being held up on the march to the barn, Tony's buckskin horse was yanking down on the reins, fighting the bit. The handsome rider's eyes went to the picks and shovels on the packhorses, and he pointed to them with his lips like an Indian. A knowing grin was spreading across his face. "Looking for treasure, eh?"

Walter Landis, who'd known this young man since he was a baby, and his parents and grandparents too on their place fifteen miles down the Piedra, replied with his best poker face, "Just seein' the country, Tony, just seein' the country."

Cloyd added, "We dig a lot of worms for fishing."

Tony Archuleta's thick black eyebrows rose, and he said, "Goldfish, no?"

Cloyd liked this man.

"The direction you're heading, let me guess . . . maybe you're going to dig some worms up at *la Ventana*?"

The old man laughed through his nose, snorting like a horse.

Tony Archuleta leaned forward, cupped his lips, and spoke in a hoarse stage whisper. "You know the old Spanish sheepherders called the Window *el Portal del Diablo*—'the Devil's Gateway.' Lot of bad storms up there, lots of unusual things that have happened to people looking for that treasure. You be careful, now. . . ."

Walter Landis winked and promised, "We'll be careful."

"You won't find Spanish treasure up there," Tony added good-naturedly. "Sixto Loco found it a long time ago, that's what I think."

"You just resupply your uncle?" the old man asked.

"I'll be back at least two more times. Well, I gotta go—and don't let Sixto see those picks and shovels. He's crankier than ever and he's a dead shot. The old people say he knows everything that goes on in the mountains. Some still call him *la Sombra*—'the Shadow.' "

They watched Tony go. Just before he crossed the creek, he turned and called back, "Hey, Yuta coyote! I told Sixto Loco about the hay I got for him! I told him he'd probably want to eat with his sheep this winter! Too bad I robbed you on the price!"

Cloyd was grinning, and he was repeating the name, "Sixto Loco."

"I never met him," Walter said, "but I'll sure enough

take Tony's warning to heart. Sixto Archuleta's repu-
tation was made a long, long time ago. His brother
disappeared in the mountains when they were both
young men . . . some say Sixto killed his brother and
buried him somewhere in the wilderness. I've heard
that story too about him finding treasure—they say he
killed his brother over gold."

"And he's a sheepherder?"

"Only one left in the mountains. The market's been
poor for years and years, and nobody wants the life of
a high-country shepherd—too lonely, too cold, too dangerous. A few of the families keep sheep on their home
places, but nothing like the numbers they used to winter in New Mexico and summer up in the San Juans.
Sixto's the only one left. Lives alone in the winter, with
just his dogs, at his place along the San Juan River.
Near the ghost town of Gato as I recollect; I've driven
by it now and again. It's just a shotgun shack off the
side of the old railroad bed, with pelts nailed over the
cracks in the walls. Saw him once splitting wood out
in his yard—there's no denying the man has a baleful
look in his eye. . . . Year after year, he takes his flock
back above the timberline . . . that man's been out in
the wind and the cold more than any in the country,
I'm sure."

"If he found the treasure, he would've built a better
house."

The old man stood up to go, and limped on the leg
that had been broken. "I'd agree with you, but people
have an explanation for that. They say he's just too
ornery to change his ways. There's a story I heard about
him . . . every three or four years he decides to drive

his old pickup into town—it's supposed to be about as old as its 1939 license plates. He'll drive into town with it, and when he gets pulled over for expired plates, he'll say, 'Throw me in jail! It's nice and warm in there, and you'll have to feed me!' "

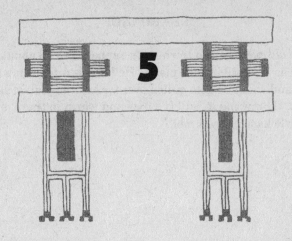

5

In the night Walter had a coughing fit. He coughed so hard, he couldn't stop until he got out of his bedroll and went outside to get a drink of water. Cloyd was alarmed. Walter had to be eighty years old, and he was sick. The thin air was hard on him, and tonight they were camping at 11,600 feet, just below the tree line in the Rincon La Osa. The map showed the Window at 12,857 feet. Where the old man wanted to look for the lost mine, the storms would be fierce and the air even thinner than here. Should they be heading for "the Devil's Gateway"?

"Should've brought some water into the tent with me," Walter said when he came back inside. "I'll remember next time."

"Maybe we should turn back," Cloyd said. "Maybe it's too high up here."

"We'll rest up here another day. If I can't do it, I won't. This'll pass. I feel like a fat pony in high oats up here. You'll see."

The "fat pony" felt better in the morning, even better the next day. Early in the morning they started for the Continental Divide, and when they reached it the sky was bursting with peaks, hundreds of them. The old man said he'd better sit down or he was going to fly away like a kite, and so they got off their horses. Cloyd pointed out the Needles, a riot of peaks close at hand to the west, all rock and sky and straight up and down. He pointed south to the mesas of New Mexico, and southwest to the vague shapes of the Chuska Mountains of Arizona.

Then they looked east along the Divide. The old man's eyes were moist. Cloyd couldn't tell if it wasn't only from the wind. Walter had his eye on a lone giant of a mountain only a few miles away. "That's got to be *el Cerro de la Piramide*, as the book calls it, but where the heck is *la Ventana*?"

"In the ridge between us and the Pyramid," Cloyd said. "We can't see the Window because we're lined straight up with that ridge. But look over here."

Cloyd was looking at an immense spur off the Divide that stuck out to the north in the direction of the Rio Grande. He pointed it out to the old man. "From there you'd be looking straight across to the Window. Remember how it said in the book, you could see the Window from the mine?"

They made their camp a thousand feet down off the Divide on the Rio Grande side, fifteen minutes' ride below the timberline and at the head of East Ute Creek's long meadow. They pitched their sheepherder tent at the edge of the meadow, with the forest at their back and a splendid view of the Rio Grande Pyramid towering above all the big country. "Only thing this camp's lacking is a view of the Window," the old man said. "I know it's up there somewhere."

By their campfire the old man brought out his treasure book and began to read from the chapter called *"La Mina Perdida de la Ventana."*

" 'To the Spaniards adventuring north from Santa Fe and Taos,' " the old man began, " 'the San Juan Mountains in the Continental Divide's east-west bend must have taken on the appearance of a majestic wall spiked with hundreds of towering peaks, clad in a forbidding mantle of white much of the year.' "

The old man paused for breath. His eyes were sparkling with excitement in the reflected light of the fire. Cloyd liked the way he read. He liked the way the old man's voice trembled not so much with the thin air, though that was part of it, as with the effects of his gold fever, all stirred up by the closeness of the legendary mine.

" 'The Spanish of the 1700s knew from two hundred years' experience in the New World that such a range was likely to contain fabulous lodes of gold and silver. Of all the landmarks in these mountains, none rivaled the combination of one lone peak with the appearance of a pyramid, and the massive notch in the ridge to its west. The mountain they named *el Cerro de la Pyramide,* the notch *la Ventana.*' "

Cloyd knew this passage by heart, and so did the old man. But here, with the Pyramid itself looming above them, the words seemed to reverberate with power, as if it might really be true that the Spanish had toiled somewhere very close to here and left a fabulous treasure behind.

Walter handed the book over for Cloyd's turn, saying "I just wish we'd caught a glimpse of that Window even once today."

Cloyd said, "Now we're too close underneath it."

" 'The Spanish had been in nearby New Mexico since Cor-o-na-do's conquest of 1540,' " Cloyd began. Once he'd caught on to reading, he could pronounce almost anything. But he had to go slow. " 'By the early 1700s they were bringing gold secretly out of southwestern Colorado's Ute frontier. The Spanish operated in secret to avoid paying "the king's fifth." ' "

Cloyd stopped reading and let his eyes show that he didn't understand the meaning.

"One-fifth of all treasure from the New World went right back to the king in Spain," Walter explained. "No wonder they were mining on the sly."

" 'They also operated in secret,' " Cloyd read, " 'because they feared the Utes.' " This part always brought a smile to his face. " 'It was known to the Utes that the Spanish made a practice of taking slaves among the Navajos and the pueblo peoples, mostly women and children to work in their households.' "

"Now you," Cloyd said, and showed the place to the old man.

"Let's remember to pay close attention," Walter said. "Listen hard for clues. It says, 'A group of six Spaniards and Frenchmen discovered a lode of high-grade gold ore in 1750 and worked their mine over the span of twenty summers. The ore was carried on mule trains toward Taos or Santa Fe, but before it was carried out each fall it was hidden in three major caches and a number of minor caches in the district around the mine. Two of the minor caches have been found by treasure hunters, one on West Ute Creek in the summer of 1936, the other on Middle Ute Creek in 1937. The ore from both proved amazingly rich; both caches had been marked by an intricate pattern of tree blazes and rock cairns. The mine itself was located west of the Window—' "

"Wait a minute," Cloyd said. "What pattern? Why doesn't it say?"

"Just doesn't," Walter said with a shrug, and threw a few more sticks onto the fire. "Maybe if the writer knew, he would've found the treasure instead of only spending years looking for it."

Cloyd's old doubts were coming back. Maybe it's just a story, he thought, but he didn't say so.

As convinced as ever, Walter continued, his voice eager with excitement: " 'The mine itself was located west of the Window, which could be seen from the entrance of the mine. Over a period of twenty years the original miners made themselves rich and also made enemies of the Utes. When the Utes surprised them and the end came—' "

"It doesn't say what they did to make enemies of the Utes," Cloyd interrupted. "It should've said that."

"You're right, it should have told about that. Probably never got written down anywhere. Anyhow, we're just getting to this part here where you've been reading it so careful, your eyes almost wore the print off the page."

"Where?"

"Look, right here."

"That's just a smudge."

"Spooked me too," the old man said with a wink. "It's about Aguilar and the skeletons: 'Some of the miners died and others escaped, but none ever returned. The mine itself was never rediscovered, except perhaps by a Spanish sheepherder named Doneciano Aguilar in 1908. A teller of tales, one night he told his fellows at camp of spying two skeletons through an opening in a ledge at the foot of a cliff, in the vicinity of the Window. He said he hadn't gone in to investigate because of the darkness and his fear of "*los espiritus de los antiguos*— the spirits of the ancients.*" When Aguilar was laughed at, he resolved never to tell the location of the mine. Convicted of a murder the following year, he was sent to the state penitentiary in Santa Fe to serve a life sentence.' "

Walter closed the book. The fire had burned low once again. "Cloyd, do you realize," the old man said slowly, emphasizing every word, "no one has ever searched for those three major caches with a metal detector the caliber of ours."

Cloyd nodded agreeably, acknowledging the old man's faith in his secret piece of equipment.

"This Cachefinder of ours is stuffed full of microchips and all that new computer technology! Scans deeper than any metal detector ever made, anywhere in the world!"

Cloyd stretched and smiled, and shivered with the night cold. At least Walter didn't have any doubts.

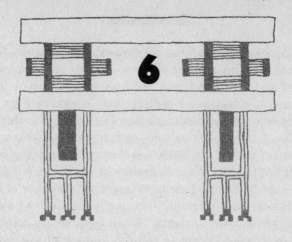

6

The next morning the old man studied the lay of the mountains and pored over the maps, thinking it all out. "We know the mine should be up behind us somewhere," he said. "It should be on that slope of the ridge above us, facing the Window. We can't see the tailings because they would have dropped them over a ledge, mixed them into a rockslide to disguise the location of the mine. But we're not looking for the mine so much as for the caches of high-grade ore, the ones they left behind when the survivors skedaddled for Santa Fe. Now where would you look for those caches, Cloyd?"

Cloyd had been thinking about it. "If I was them, I wouldn't want to try to hide anything up on that ridge—too much rock. It would be easier to hide the ore down in the trees. The digging would be a lot easier."

"Same thing I'm thinking. Maybe you've got a nose for treasure after all."

"Besides," Cloyd added, "the book said there were markings on rocks and markings on *trees*."

"We'll keep our eyes out for those grizzlies too," Walter declared. "That mother and her three cubs."

"Brown, cocoa, and gray-black," Cloyd remembered.

"Grizzlies and gold," the old man sang, "that's you and me, Cloyd. Grizzlies and gold."

Cloyd was glad they weren't going to have to comb the high, steep slopes above for treasure. They couldn't camp up there. The horses had no pasture up there. Walter would never survive trying to cling to those elk trails up on the ledges.

Mostly, Cloyd thought, Walter needs to nurse that cough. Down in the trees we'll be protected from the weather.

Every morning Walter took off with his Cachefinder, scanning the forest floor back from the meadow. For several days Cloyd went with him, and then he started to stray in search of old Spanish blazes or piles of rocks that might mark one of the caches the old man was looking for. But really, he didn't believe in the gold. Even if the story was true, two hundred and more years was a long time for a tree to heal an axe wound. The marked trees might have even died and returned to the soil. Two hundred years provided plenty of time for a little pile of rocks to fall down.

His eyes were searching tree bark for high claw marks that might have been left by a grizzly, and searching the ground for tracks with claws far forward of the footpad.

On an aspen, as high as his hand could reach, he

found the claw marks of a bear. These marks didn't prove anything. A black bear, he knew, could reach that high or higher.

But when he found a pile of bear scat, full of seeds, bits of bone, and strands of hair, Cloyd had to wonder. Could a black bear leave this big a dropping? He kept a segment in a plastic bag and brought it back to show to Walter.

"Wish I could tell you," Walter said. "I just don't know."

It began to rain every day, by two in the afternoon at the latest. Sometimes they were both back in camp, and through the fold in the door of the sheepherder tent, they would watch the hail dance. Other times the weather would catch them away from camp, and they would each wait it out before returning. The temperature could drop thirty degrees in less than thirty minutes, but Cloyd was ready for it. His cold-weather clothing and his rain gear were so much better than what he'd had the year before. The old man had taken him to the Pine Needle Mountaineering store in Durango and had written a big check. His red rain shell with both top and trousers wouldn't allow any moisture in, even though it would let his sweat out. His clothes were staying dry.

Later in the afternoon the sun would come back out, and they would dry their wet things on the big boulder, knee-high and flat like a table, out in the meadow halfway to the creek.

Five days had passed in their camp, and Walter had worked the trees on both sides as far as he could reach downstream. They'd dug a few holes where the old man had heard a hopeful signal, and then they filled the holes back in. "Let's move downstream a mile or so," the old man suggested. "Those caches must be just out of our reach."

Cloyd liked the new camp better. It was closer to the fishing. In the late afternoons after the thunderstorms died down, he rode Blueboy a few miles down the creek to the beaver ponds to find fish for dinner.

Every night it was freezing now, and the tundra grasses and flowers were turning red and gold.

Mornings he rose early, and his breath spouted jets of vapor. It was never long before the old man hooked the Cachefinder's sending and receiving unit to his belt, adjusted the headphones, and started out in search of treasure. Every day was a new adventure for the old man, mint-full of promise. With Walter Landis, the harder he searched, the more the search possessed him, and the more he became convinced that the moment of discovery was imminent. From a distance, you couldn't tell that he was keeping the circular search coil slightly above the ground. It looked like he was out vacuuming the meadow or the mountainsides.

In the afternoons Walter would tire of being on his feet, and he'd pick at little cracks in the stream bottom's bedrock, cleaning all the grooves and cracks with a screwdriver bent at right angles near the tip. The old man called it "crevice mining," but to Cloyd it looked like Walter was an old dentist who'd just gone crazy.

It didn't seem as crazy when the old man brought him a nugget the size of a raisin that had been caught in one of the cracks. Walter Landis was so excited,

Cloyd could picture what he'd be like if he actually found a big treasure. His heart might not be able to take it. He might die on the spot out of pure happiness.

At the edge of a melt pond, below snowbanks that had survived the summer in the shadows, Cloyd found bear tracks in the mud. They showed five toes but lacked the grizzly's long claws. Nearby, fresh bear scat. Even if it wasn't a grizzly, he wanted to track this bear.

The trail led down the mountain into the timber, where the bear had stopped to dig up a squirrel's cache and to overturn a log for the ants and grubs underneath. Cloyd tracked the bear upslope now, far from any trail, and thought he'd lost it when he emerged from the forest at the tree line. The bear wasn't above him on the open, grassy slopes as he'd hoped. But when he crouched and then crawled up to the very top of the Divide, with the wind blowing stiffly in his face, there the black bear was, not thirty feet away, sitting on its haunches and sniffing the wind.

The bear couldn't see him and didn't catch his scent either, until the wind shifted a little. All it took was a look over its shoulder, and the bear exploded in flight down the mountainside. The black bear didn't stop running until it had reached the timber more than a mile below. Cloyd had read about this, how fast a bear could run, but he'd never seen it himself.

As if out of the sky, a woman appeared over the grassy slope of the Divide. She was coming his way.

As the hiker approached, he could see that her eyes were shaped like his. Almond-eyed, high-cheekboned, with dark, braided hair that fell almost to her waist, she had to be Indian, though she didn't look very much like a Ute or Navajo. She was carrying a big pack, but she wasn't bent under it. Her legs were sinewy and strong, and she came striding toward him across the alpine carpet of short wildflowers, out of the blue sky and billowing white clouds. From her neck hung the largest pair of binoculars he had ever seen and a camera with an extra-long lens.

"That bear was sure surprised," the woman said in greeting, with a smile at her lips. "You could've almost tapped him on the shoulder. I've been watching you. You're a good tracker." Her eyes were black, and her chin delicate like his sister's. He guessed she might be the age his mother would have been, had she lived.

"I'm just learning," he said.

She didn't offer her hand, and Cloyd was glad of that. She was curious about him, but her eyes didn't try to know him all at once. "I'm Cloyd Atcitty," he offered.

"I'm Ursa."

She took off her pack and sat quietly, and admired the view. Her eyes were on the Pyramid and the Window. Close at her throat, a small, flattened turquoise bear hung suspended from a delicate gold chain.

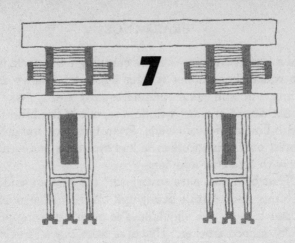

7

"Your necklace," Cloyd said. "It's a bear."

The Indian woman who'd appeared out of the sky smiled a smile that reminded him even more of his sister, who was curious and did well in school and liked to laugh. The woman touched her bear charm and said, "It's for my name, Ursa. My name means 'bear.'"

Everything about her was filling him with surprise and awe. Yet she was easy to talk to. "What are you doing up here?" he asked her. "Where did you come from?"

She laughed. "I was about to ask you the same question. But you asked first. This morning I came from the head of Snowslide Canyon, and I'm looking for grizzly bears in these mountains."

Ursa was watching his eyes to see his reaction. She could see how keenly he was listening.

Cloyd asked quickly, "Have you found any?"

The woman with the long braid shook her head. "Of course, I've only been trying for three weeks. There've been teams from the U.S. Fish and Wildlife Service looking all summer. . . . They've given up; they're all gone now. There's only me left, and a couple of game wardens who are somewhere west of that mountain right now."

She was pointing toward the Rio Grande Pyramid.

"Are you from around here?" Cloyd asked doubtfully.

Ursa brought out two granola bars and gave him one. "I'm a wildlife biologist—I research grizzlies. I teach at the University of Montana in Missoula. Unfortunately, I'm running out of time down here on my grizzly search—I have to be back in the classroom nine days from now."

Cloyd was wondering how much she knew. Had there been more sightings? "How come everybody's looking for grizzlies?" he asked her.

Ursa paused, looking out over the mountains, nibbling at her granola bar. Cloyd had already wolfed his. He was pleased that the storm in the Needles didn't look like it was heading their way. The sun was shining on this conversation, which he didn't want to end.

"I'll go back to the beginning," Ursa said with a smile. "Last summer there was a grizzly bear killed in these mountains. It was the first grizzly confirmed in Colorado since the early 1950s. When people think of grizzlies, they think of a few places in Wyoming and Montana, but not Colorado. The story even ran in papers around the country—people were amazed. It

caught people's imagination to think of grizzlies surviving in Colorado all this time."

"Grizzlies? You said *grizzlies*. There's more than that
one, for sure?"

Ursa's black eyes reflected hope and doubt at the
same time. "The only evidence we have so far is the
word of the outfitter who killed the grizzly last
summer. He claims he saw a grizzly with three cubs
this May, over in that drainage there. . . ." The grizzly
woman, as Cloyd now thought of her, was pointing to
the Rincon La Vaca, below the Pyramid on the Pine
River side. "But I'm not sure I believe him, even if he
is fully qualified to tell grizzlies apart from black bears.
This guy goes to Alaska to hunt grizzlies every year.
He's not exactly a friend of bears."

Mention of the red-haired man was making Cloyd
sick and angry. The red-haired man always seemed to
be the big man in the middle of things.

"No one who knows bears and knows his back-
ground really believes his version of what happened
last summer, when the grizzly supposedly surprised
him. . . ."

Cloyd's heart was beating fast. Not everybody had
believed Rusty's story.

"There was someone who might know what really
did happen," the grizzly woman said. "There was supposed to have been a boy, a Ute boy, who was there
when the bear was killed. . . ."

Cloyd's face was blank, like a mask. He would let
her talk.

Suddenly she stopped and looked at him. "You," she
said. "You are that boy, aren't you?"

He nodded. It was time to tell her his story. She wanted to know, and he would tell her.

As he was about to begin, she said, "Start from the beginning."

Cloyd wondered where the beginning was. His mother, who died getting him born? His father, in a sleep he would never waken from in the hospital in Window Rock? His grandmother, who raised him; the group home in Durango?

"I found a bearstone once," he said, pointing at the charm at her throat with a twist of his lips.

He was sparing with his words, but Cloyd told her more of himself, of his true feelings, than he had ever told anyone before. He wanted to tell his story to this woman. In addition to being the grizzly woman, it felt like she was his sister, his grandmother, the mother he never knew. He told her about Walter Landis, the farm, and the gold mine, and he told her the true story of what had really happened when Rusty killed the grizzly.

"I'm not surprised," Ursa said when he was done. Her voice sounded tired and sad. "It's an old story, the mountain man killing the thing he loves. Indian people have known this lesson for a long time. The People know that the hunter who only takes and gives nothing in return will one day wake up to find that all the animals have vanished. This is what comes from not recognizing that people and animals are all relatives in the spirit world."

It was strange, how closely her words echoed his grandmother's. "Do you really believe there's a spirit world?" he asked her.

Ursa's eyes shone with conviction. "Oh, yes," she said softly.

It made him feel good to hear her talk.

"Cloyd, I only hope Rusty Owens was telling the truth about the mother and cubs. Let me tell you what's at stake. . . . If any of us can prove there are still grizzlies in Colorado, in this Weminuche Wilderness, it means they'll be given the greatest possible protection under the Endangered Species Act, and most likely more will be brought in, to insure a breeding population."

At first Cloyd doubted he could have heard right. This news was almost too wonderful to believe. "That's true?" he asked her, not with a smile, but with almost desperate hope.

"True," the grizzly woman said. "Prove one, they'll bring others."

He could hardly wait to tell the old man about that. "Can you camp with us tonight?" Cloyd asked her, looking away as he said it. He didn't want her to leave.

"Sounds great," she said. "And I'd love to meet your friend."

On their way down to the camp on East Ute Creek, Cloyd told her about the bear scat he'd found. Ursa was listening carefully. "I'll take some hairs from it," she told him. "In the laboratory, they'll be able to tell if it's black bear or grizzly. The chromosome structures in the DNA are different."

Cloyd led her down the mountainside. Behind him, he heard nothing, she walked so quietly. He could learn to go as softly. One thing she had said above all others stuck in his mind and kept repeating itself: "Prove one, they'll bring others."

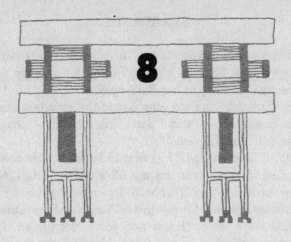

It was a special time, this evening with the grizzly woman in camp. Walter had baked a peach cobbler in the Dutch oven, and Ursa and Cloyd both ate seconds. She liked peaches and peach cobbler just as much as he did. They were finishing up their cobbler, and the old man was pouring coffee out of the old enamel pot. "Nothing like coffee out in the fresh air," Walter was saying. "Never tastes better. Warms up the old bones. Cloyd, you sure are a lucky fellow. Imagine meeting someone way back here that's as keen on bears as you are. . . ."

The woman was eyeing both of them fondly, this unlikely combination of a Ute boy and an old white rancher. She'd been charmed by the grizzled farmer-turned-prospector and his fascination with gold, his eagerness to speak of the excitement of the search, his instinctive reluctance to tell in detail of the treasure he was after. She was sipping her coffee, and the firelight was dancing in her dark eyes.

"If I might," the old man asked the grizzly woman in a formal tone, "and I don't mean to pry ... but is Ursa your entire name?"

"It is," she replied. "I gave it to myself at the time I decided to make grizzlies my life's work. The name I grew up with was Elizabeth Torsness. I grew up in southeast Alaska. My mother is Tlingit and my father's people were some Tlingit and some Norwegian. His great-grandfather came from Norway during the Alaska gold rush."

Alaska, Cloyd thought. The name had magic and power. Alaska was big and beautiful, he knew, but mostly what it meant to him was bears. Alaska meant huge bears.

" 'Kling-it'?" the old man repeated. "I don't believe I've heard of Kling-its." He stroked his beard with great seriousness. "Heard of Kling-*ons*—Cloyd and I went to one of them *Star Trek* movies."

The grizzly woman had a good laugh. "That's the way it sounds, but it has a funny spelling. Begins with a T instead of a K. We're one of the tribes that carves the totem poles. We didn't for a long time, but now we're starting to again."

Walter was shaking his head in wonder and pouring himself another cup of coffee. He held it in his hands, letting the hot cup warm them before it warmed him inside. "I always wanted to see Alaska," he said. "I guess I never will."

"Did you see bears where you grew up?" Cloyd asked her.

"Bears were our only neighbors," Ursa replied. "They were grizzly bears, though in Alaska people mostly call them brown bears or especially 'brownies.' I grew up on Admiralty Island, a big island off the coast. My father was a fisherman and he built a float house about halfway between the mouths of two streams. The brownies fished too, and when the salmon were running you could see as many as twenty around the falls on one of those creeks."

"Twenty grizzlies in one place," the old man marveled. "Imagine that, Cloyd."

Cloyd was imagining, as Ursa was filling in the details. "The falls were only about six feet high," she said. "Bears would stake out their favorite fishing holes, either in the stream right below the falls or right on the edge of the falls themselves. Now and then they would have terrible fights over the best spots . . . but grizzlies can take as well as give horrible wounds. They have amazing powers of healing."

"And you would see them catch the fish?" Cloyd asked.

"Oh, yes. I especially liked to watch the ones standing on the lip of the falls. They'd just hang their heads out there—sometimes they'd grab one in midair. I watched them all the time. A brownie can eat a hundred pounds of salmon in a day. There's so much food up there . . . that's why they grow bigger than Rocky Mountain grizzlies."

Cloyd was having trouble picturing one thing. "How can you get close enough to watch them . . . without getting hurt?"

"Don't get me wrong," Ursa said. "Grizzlies can be dangerous. . . . But people and bears have been sharing

51

those salmon streams for thousands of years. It's a matter of respecting the bears' dominance, knowing how to act around them, knowing the distance that's comfortable for them."

"How close?" the old man wondered, his eyes wide.

"At the creeks, a few hundred feet. They were used to us. It was close enough—they looked enormous to me. Quite a few of them weighed upward of a thousand pounds. We'd see them all the time on the tidal flats around our house. They'd loll around like hound dogs."

"Holy cow!" Walter exclaimed. "I thought I could tell a whopper, Cloyd. Her actual life story's taller'n a whopper!"

Ursa had a sparkle in her eye and Cloyd wondered for a moment if she was making all this up, but he didn't think so.

"Sometimes people came to visit," she continued. "They'd want to see the bears fishing. They were uncomfortable if my father didn't carry a weapon along, so he carried a hefty stick just to make them feel better."

"Did he ever use it?" asked Cloyd, who was anxious to know more about how dangerous grizzlies were.

She smiled. "If a thousand-pound bear charged at thirty miles an hour...,"the grizzly woman calculated, "that stick wouldn't have seemed like much of a weapon. No, he never used it, but he did get hurt once by a bear. It was a bear that was new to the creek. The bear rushed him and broke his collarbone and three ribs. . . ."

The grizzly woman's face filled with emotion as she paused, remembering. "It was my mother who saved my father from a worse mauling, or even being killed.

Was that bear ever surprised when she opened her umbrella in his face! I'll never forget the look in that bear's eyes and how fast it ran off."

"Well, I'll be busted to flinderjigs!" Walter exclaimed, with a quick slap to his knee. "My, my . . . And how about you, Ursa? This research that you do among the grizzlies in Wyoming and Montana . . . have you ever been hurt?"

Ursa gave a few raps on the log she was sitting on. "Not so far. I'm very careful not to blunder between a mother and her cubs, but I do get a lot closer than hikers who are wearing bells, making noise, giving bears the opportunity to vanish without ever being seen. I need to get close to make my notes and to take pictures and movies. Grizzlies get used to me being around, and they'll go about their business. But I've been charged a few times over the years. . . ."

Now Cloyd's eyes were as wide as saucers. "You were?"

"Grizzlies will bluff you into giving them the space they feel they need. The scary part is, their bluffs don't look like bluffs in the least. It's the scariest thing in your life. If the bear not only stands up, but woofs several times . . . if you hear a popping sound of the jaws, and the bear lays its ears back—look out."

"Good lord," the old man whispered hoarsely.

Cloyd felt like he was there, and one of those bears was charging him.

Ursa's teeth were clenched. "If you turn and run," she said, "you'll probably get mauled. In a short burst, they're faster than a racehorse."

"Then what do you do?" Cloyd wondered.

"You try to make yourself look as big as possible,

without making any threatening gestures. But don't look the bear in the eye. You talk softly and apologetically. If it charges, it'll probably stop before it gets to you. Or sometimes it'll run right past you."

The old man was pulling hard on his beard. "Gives me chills just thinking about it!"

She shrugged. "I try to keep in mind that I'm statistically much more at risk driving on the highway. So, the more time I spend in grizzly country and out of my car, the longer I'll live, statistically speaking."

Cloyd could tell that Walter liked this woman. Cloyd liked watching the old man's face as he listened to her stories. Walter said with a grin, "Must be hard to recall those statistics when a grizzly's charging. . . ."

"They are simply awesome creatures," Ursa replied. "You never forget how powerful they are and how deadly they could be. The amazing thing is, ordinarily they're ferocious only when attacked. They don't take kindly to being killed, and when they are being killed, 'they're hard to put down' as the hunters in Alaska often say. They can do a lot of damage as they're dying."

For a while, no one spoke. Each turned within. The fire had burned low, and the chill of the late August night was reaching their bones.

Cloyd wondered if he could be as brave as Ursa. He wished he could see another grizzly. Even just one more, just a glimpse.

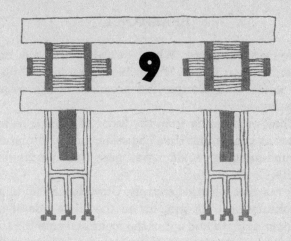

Cloyd stuffed as much as he could into his big daypack and he followed the grizzly woman up and out of East Ute Creek, over Gunsight Pass, and into the Ute Lakes Basin, a fifteen-mile-wide shelf in the shape of a crescent above the timberline.

The grizzly woman was leading him across the tundra, below the boulder fields and above the swath of mountain willows that covered the entire basin like a living blanket. She would stop and scan those willows with her high-powered binoculars, and she would scan the meadows of Middle Ute Creek miles below.

Walter had said, "Go with her. Maybe you'll find the bears."

Cloyd was happy to be out searching with Ursa, yet he'd gone with misgivings, knowing he might be away several days. When he'd left the old man alone the year before, Walter had blown himself up in his mine, even though he'd promised not to do any blasting.

They were eating from the lunch of dried fruit and nuts and cheese that Ursa had set out on the miniature, ground-hugging wildflowers, pink and purple and white.

A marmot whistled sharply. Cloyd looked up to see a solitary bull elk grazing on the other side of the boulder field. In and out of the rocks and onto the tundra, a mother ptarmigan and her half-grown young were pecking along in their mottled summer plumage.

"The Tlingit believe that grizzlies can know the future," Ursa said. "They believe that grizzlies can understand our speech and know what we are saying about them, even from great distances. Do the Utes believe this also?"

"I don't know," Cloyd said. "Maybe they did, I don't know."

"Some of the tribes would hunt grizzlies. Others wouldn't, like mine up in Alaska and many of them in your part of the country, because they believed that grizzlies are half-human. The ones who hunted grizzlies did so with great respect, hoping to gain power from them. Power to be used in battle or to feed one's family was a good thing."

"You know about all the tribes?"

"I try to learn as much as I can," the grizzly woman said with a sigh. "I know very little compared to what there is to know, compared to what's been lost. When it comes to bears, I want to know everything. Maybe I want to know too much. Mostly, Indian women in the past were afraid of bears, afraid that bears would come out of the woods and take them back with them to be their wives. The Tlingit tell a story about people being related to bears. It's called 'The Woman Who Married a Bear.' "

Cloyd had to think about this. He asked her, "How did it happen in the story?"

"A girl didn't follow the rules about the distance that people and bears should keep along the salmon streams. She was picking berries and got separated from her family. A young man came along, a handsome young man, and they began talking."

"Was it . . . the bear?"

The grizzly woman nodded. "But in her eyes it was a young man. In the old times, there was magic that went back and forth between people and bears. People could look at bears and see people, and bears could look at people and see bears."

Again, the grizzly woman was echoing his grandmother's words. It was strange and wonderful to think that two tribes so far apart would tell stories so much alike.

"Her children," Cloyd wondered. "Were they bears or people?"

A smile played at the grizzly woman's lips. "Who knows? Maybe they were whichever was in the minds of the ones looking at them. But the story says that after her brothers came to the den and killed her husband, she returned to her people and lived with them until her brothers made fun of her for being mated to a bear. At that moment she and her children turned into bear and cubs. She killed her brothers, and all the people learned a great lesson of respect as she fled into the woods with her children."

"That's a good story," Cloyd said.

"There's wisdom in all those old stories."

"Maybe the bears around here heard you tell all this," Cloyd said with a chuckle.

Ursa laughed a bright, musical laugh. "That grizzly with her three cubs—maybe she'd like those old stories. She might come a little closer and give us a look."

At their camp, he wanted to ask her something. "You said Indian women were afraid of bears. How come you're different?"

"My mother wanted me to have a bear as a spirit helper. She had heard that the people down the coast, the Kwakiutl, knew how to get their daughters the power of the grizzly as food gatherer. They believed that if the right forepaw of a bear is placed on the palm of the right hand of an infant girl, she will be successful in picking berries and digging clams. So my mother did this with me."

A *spirit helper*, Cloyd thought. He'd never heard this expression before. "How did they get a spirit helper, the people in the old days?"

"By dreaming," she replied. "All across the continent, people believed that when they dreamed, their souls left their bodies and traveled about in the spirit world. In a dream you could see something that would normally be invisible. You could even visit the spirit home of the bears."

"My grandmother talked about spirit bears," he said,

and then he told her what had happened at the Bear Dance, when he had lifted out of his body and up above the Bear Dance and had looked down.

She listened carefully, and when he was done, she said, "What did you learn when you were out there that you could bring back?"

He thought hard, and then he said, "I guess nothing."

"Well, at least you can dream," she said, her dark eyes full of fire. "That's a great thing. On his dream journey, a hunter might learn a design for his quiver that pleased the animals, or he might meet the spirit keeper of the animal he was hunting and be shown a good place to hunt. When a dream came true, it was said that you *found* your dream."

Cloyd stretched out, with his hand behind his head, and looked at the stars. It was a lucky thing he had met this woman. These things that she knew, they were things he wanted to know.

"I wish I'd seen the Ute Bear Dance," Ursa said, "but I've only read about it. Do a man and a woman still appear at the end of the endurance dance, dressed in the skins of bears?"

Cloyd was shaking his head. "I don't think so. I never saw that."

"Maybe they don't do that part anymore. It was to show that the bears had heard the people's good wishes, that they had wakened from their hibernation and were going out into the world again. It was always held at the end of the winter, to help wake up the bears and help bring spring."

"It's late in May now," Cloyd said. "Memorial Day weekend."

"Show me how to do the bear dance," she urged.

He got to his feet, but then he hesitated. "It would be better if you could hear the sounds. Let me try to make the sounds for you."

Cloyd found two sticks, and he whittled one smooth and notched the other, carefully and deliberately. The grizzly woman was done with speaking now, and watched with great interest as he whittled the sticks.

When he was ready Cloyd began to make the rasping thunder, and he was pleased that the sound coming off the sticks was much like it should be. He demonstrated the three steps forward, three steps back, and then explained, "The woman has to ask the man to dance."

She came to him, and tugged on the bottom of his rain jacket, and smiled a shy, girlish smile, just like a girl of fourteen.

At first their steps were small and slow ones. He stepped toward her as she retreated, then she stepped toward him as he fell back.

Ursa began taking bigger steps, springing to the rhythm of his rasp. Her long braid was flying as they leaped back and forth, back and forth. After they'd danced that way awhile, he showed her his favorite form of the bear dance. Side by side, they faced in opposite directions with his hand around her waist, her hand around his. He couldn't play the rasp, but their feet didn't need to hear the beat to keep to it. The beat seemed to be coming up out of the earth, way back out of the life of the People.

After they danced, he played the rasp for a long time, and then she played the rasp for a long time.

Miles down in the timber, in the deep spruce forest back from the long meadow down Middle Ute Creek, a bear heard the unusual sound of the growler sticks. She had an innate curiosity perhaps greater than any other animal's, and she was highly curious about this sound. She had spent a good part of the afternoon on a daybed she'd scratched in the earth, after feeding in the morning from the carcass of a cougar-killed deer she'd dug up from under its shallow covering of boughs and spruce needles. Following the mountain lion had paid off for her and her three cubs, and when the cat had returned to feed again, it had been a simple matter to chase it off.

Curious about this unusual night sound, she led her cubs up the mountain, close enough that she could identify the forms of two human beings, both sitting cross-legged, one making the sound with two sticks. It was curious that this sound came from two human beings. She went to great lengths to avoid people, yet sometimes when she felt safe she would watch them. This sound was new and interesting, and it sounded nothing like the noises that human beings made. It sounded something like thunder, and something like bears. Her three cubs, sitting on their haunches in a straight row, listened with great interest as well. The four of them listened until the sound stopped, and then they turned silently into the night.

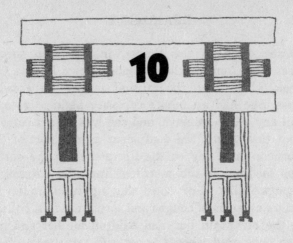

10

It was Cloyd who spotted them, in the morning, as he glassed all he could see of the tundra fields above the chest-high willow thickets of the Ute Lakes Basin. Along the edge of a boulder field that seemed to flow like a glacier off the Continental Divide, he found them with the grizzly woman's powerful binoculars. At first he thought he hadn't seen them at all, that his mind was tricking him with his greatest wish, but he blinked and held the binoculars as steadily as he could and counted the cubs that were lined up, watching their mother dig. One, two, three.

Even from this distance, over half a mile, Cloyd could catch the silver sheen on their mother's fur as she dug furiously in the tundra. He knew she was a grizzly. He could even make out the hump on her back just behind her neck. There were stones flying from her claws. She seized a large stone with both forepaws and hurled it aside. Carefully, before he took the field glasses from his eyes, he noted all the landmarks around the spot, the unique pattern of the Divide and the rock flow and the tundra.

"Ursa," he said as calmly as he could, and then he gave her a tug on her sleeve. He showed her where to look.

As Ursa focused the binoculars, a smile came to her lips. She looked a long time in silence. "Cloyd," she whispered, "we've brought each other luck."

They packed quickly, and then he followed as she used the wind and the shape of the land to find a place where they could watch without the bear catching their scent. "It's good she has three cubs," Ursa whispered. "Two's more common. Grizzlies have young only every other year at best, and cubs often die."

The woman made no sound as she moved toward the spot she had selected. Cloyd imitated her every move. He only hoped, when they gained the spot, that the bears would not have left.

He wasn't disappointed. Alongside the grizzly woman, he inched forward on his belly into a cluster of rocks that would shield them from view. When the moment came, he found the mother grizzly digging as vigorously as ever. She had excavated a pit five feet deep and eight to ten feet across. Now Cloyd didn't need the binoculars. He could even see the dished-out shape of her broad forehead.

The dirt was flying, and so were the stones. The bear flung a rock as big as a basketball over her shoulder.

The cubs were no longer lined up and watching. They'd fallen into a three-way boxing, wrestling, and chewing match.

Brown, cocoa, and gray-black, just as Rusty had said. Their mother would stop and look around every minute or so, constantly on the alert.

"The cubs look healthy," the grizzly woman whispered. "Seven months old, probably fifty pounds."

Ursa began taking pictures—two, three—very quickly. "For the proof we need, I have to risk disturbing them," she said, and indeed the mother grizzly stood up on two legs and sniffed the air, looked their way. Had the bear heard the camera's shutter?

Maybe, but maybe not. After a long minute, the grizzly went back to her digging. The grizzly woman didn't take any more pictures. She had her proof. No one could mistake the shape of the mother grizzly's head, the silver-tipped fur, the hump above her shoulders, the long claws on her front feet.

Suddenly the cubs were seizing upon small animals—three or four of them, quite alive—that their mother was throwing up and out of the pit. "Pikas," the grizzly woman said. Cloyd recognized the small rock rabbits that Walter called conies. Several minutes later their mother's mouth came up with a nest of squirming baby conies, spilling them out onto the dirt for her cubs.

The grizzly moved away from the rocks onto the open tundra and began to dig up the shallow runs that could be found in profusion everywhere on the spongy grass. Perfect little imitators, her cubs dug furiously on their own. Cloyd had seen the little meadow mice called voles scurrying above ground on occasion, but he hadn't realized how many could be found in a small area. And he never could have guessed how successfully a grizzly could dig them up. Within an hour the mother grizzly had caught over thirty. Some she flicked the cubs' way for them to chase in the grass. The grizzly woman said it was the bear's hearing that told her exactly where to dig.

Even when she was catching voles, the mother grizzly kept her vigilance, standing up briefly, looking around. Her sight wasn't so good, but her nose was testing the wind. The brown cub tried to nurse as she stood up, and she brushed it off as if to say, Now is not the time or the place.

After noon the bear started down toward the timber. She made a daybed just inside the trees, where she lay down, nursed her cubs, and napped.

By midafternoon the bears were on the move again, and they disappeared deep into the spruce timber. Cloyd was sure he'd seen them for the last time, but the grizzly woman could detect even the faintest signs of their passage. She taught him how to tell even a grizzly's rear track apart from a black bear's. Late in the day the grizzly woman was glassing a beaver pond that sat in a little bench above West Ute Creek, and she found them again.

The big grizzly was rolling and splashing in the pond with all three cubs swimming around her. She began to root out pond lilies for them and for herself. Just like their mother, they held the lilies with both forepaws and crunched on the thick roots. When their mother at last began to swim across the pond, the cubs quickly followed. The brown one swam up onto her back and the cocoa clung to her tail end, while the gray-black swam along behind on its own.

Cloyd didn't know what it was, but suddenly he felt strange all over—on his arms, in his spine, on the back of his neck. He began to feel that he was being watched. From the corner of his eye, he tried to see if someone was watching him and Ursa as they were watching the bears. For a long time he tried to look without giving himself away, but he couldn't see a thing. The strange feeling persisted. At last he spun suddenly to see if he might spy someone or something there in the forest behind him, but he saw nothing, unless it was the suggestion of a moving shadow, a shadow he glimpsed ever so briefly.

No, he decided. It was nothing.

The mother grizzly, in her shuffling, powerful gait, ran with her head low to the ground and disappeared with her cubs into the trees. After a while, the grizzly woman said it was time to follow. At any place where bushes or boulders might have concealed the bears, Ursa angled to the side for a clear view so she wouldn't accidentally come between the grizzly and her cubs.

Cloyd and the grizzly woman were watching from the trees as the bears reappeared along the edge of the meadow of West Ute Creek. Mother and cubs were grazing on the grass and wildflowers, which surprised him. But then he remembered, from a book he'd found at school, that three-fourths of what grizzlies ate wasn't meat at all.

For a long time he watched with Ursa as the big grizzly browsed in a patch of tall cow parsnips, eating the flower tops and broad leaves and all right down to the ground. Alongside her, the cubs were clasping shredded pieces of the stalks with their forepaws and eating them like celery. At last, when the shadows grew long, their mother led them into the forest on the far side of the creek, and the bears disappeared from sight.

Tomorrow, Cloyd thought, the bears might be gone for good. But that would be all right. Ursa had the pictures. Ursa had the proof of grizzlies in the San Juan Mountains.

Prove one, they'd bring others.

In their camp that night, Cloyd had the appetite of a bear. The grizzly woman was stirring the powdered cheese into a big pot of macaroni, and now she dished out two large helpings. Then she brought a small bottle of hot sauce out of her pack and sprinkled it heavily on her macaroni and cheese. Cloyd thought he'd try some too.

The spicy dish tasted good, and it warmed him up so much that he took off his jacket and even his wool cap. He was sweating, and it felt like steam was spouting out of his ears. He felt good. "How soon will they bring more grizzlies?" he asked happily.

Ursa simply shrugged.

"But they *will* bring them back here?" Cloyd asked uncertainly.

"It's a matter of time," she said. "The law is clear. The state and federal wildlife agencies will have a responsibility now to see that this tiny grizzly population we've discovered has a future. These four are not a breeding population. They'll die out in time. There'll be studies and hearings that could take years, but it will happen."

The grizzly woman took off her cap too, and her

jacket. She sprinkled some more hot sauce onto her macaroni and cheese and broke into a smile. "I've often thought this stuff might save me from freezing to death—maybe it deserves mention in the first aid books."

"Where will they bring grizzlies from?"

"Probably from Yellowstone, in Wyoming. They're the closest. You know, Cloyd, your San Juans are the biggest stretch of wilderness south of Yellowstone. There's room for grizzlies here. That's why a few of them have been able to survive here for forty years after everyone thought they were gone."

When he said good night to her, she said, "I was thinking—just the same as bears are our spirit helpers, we're their spirit helpers too."

"I'm not sure I really have a spirit helper," Cloyd admitted. In his heart, he knew he didn't. Having a bearstone once wasn't the same as having a spirit helper. He hadn't done anything for bears. One had died because of his careless words.

"You're young," she said. "Cloyd, you could be one who fights for bears. The future looks bleak for bears, all over the world. Fights for Bears would be a good Indian name for you."

She read the doubt in his eyes. "You'll know when you have a spirit helper, Cloyd. You can dream, you already know that. You've traveled in the spirit world. I've never done that."

Ursa thought too much of him, Cloyd knew. He was only who he was. It was good enough to drift off to sleep knowing that there were still grizzlies in the mountains, that more would be brought, that they weren't going to die out after all.

BEARDANCE

He went to sleep thinking of the old man, wondering how Walter Landis was doing this night. Was he feeling well? Was his cough getting better or worse? How much was his leg hurting him? How much did it hurt to lay his body down on the ground? He thought of his sister, who was back at the boarding school in Salt Lake City, and of his grandmother. Her peaches would be ripe now on the high desert at White Mesa.

Cloyd woke remembering he had dreamed of bears in the night. It was a weird dream, not one he could find anything good about, not one he would tell the grizzly woman about. In his dream he'd been having a conversation with a bear much like the one he'd seen the summer before. The bear in his dreams reached an enormous height and never went down on all fours. They were having a conversation about the foods they liked to eat, and the bear said that his very favorite was people. "Bears don't eat human flesh," Cloyd had said, and the gigantic bear had answered, "But I do. I would like your permission to drink your blood and to eat the meat from your bones. I will leave all your bones in good condition for you to put back together."

This dream was hard to keep out of his head. He was following the grizzly woman up and out of the trees and into the brushy willows of the Ute Lakes Basin, and he kept having this crazy conversation with the dream bear over and over again. The grizzly woman was once again on the track of the mother grizzly and her three cubs. The bears were moving upslope, toward the Continental Divide, and Ursa was eager to observe them as long as she could. She had only a few more days before she had to leave to travel back to Montana and begin her classes, and she wanted to spend them observing these rarest of North America's grizzlies.

In the forest the grizzly woman pointed out logs that the mother grizzly had freshly turned over. Cloyd guessed that Ursa could track bears as well as the red-haired man, or better. Ursa was pointing out bits of mushrooms left uneaten, and holes around the roots of spruce trees where the grizzly had dug up caches of nuts. Above the timberline, there were places where the bear had dug for voles and dug up bulbs and roots.

Ursa was sure the bears were moving to the southwest, in the direction of the Continental Divide. She guessed the grizzly was going to move on to another basin. "This time of year," she said as she glassed the slopes, "they have to keep on the move. They have to lay in the fat to carry them through the times when there's hardly any food around. Oh, no!" she exclaimed suddenly.

"What is it?"

The grizzly woman had her field glasses trained on the slopes above Twin Lakes, halfway around the basin between Middle Ute Lake and Ute Lake. "Sheep," she replied. "I hope our bears are steering wide of that flock. I'm sure they can smell those sheep from miles and miles away."

Cloyd could make out the motion, the moving pattern of white on the green mountainside, each individual moving in the same direction at the same speed.

"Sheepmen hate grizzlies," Ursa said. "Some kill grizzlies on sight, endangered or no."

"Sixto Loco," Cloyd said, and he told the grizzly woman about the last sheepherder in the mountains, who was a wild man and a crack shot.

"We'll just hope our bears steer well away from him. The problem is, Cloyd, the ranchers were probably grazing sheep here in the summers for a hundred years before the Weminuche was declared a wilderness area. But you tell me, who has the greater right, sheep or grizzlies?"

Cloyd had been a shepherd too. He couldn't answer without thinking about this problem. For years, he had taken his grandmother's sheep and goats across the high desert and into the fingers of the canyons. "Do grizzlies kill sheep?" he asked.

"Some do," Ursa said. "These few who've survived so long here, they must have learned to avoid sheep and man at all costs, but it didn't used to be so rare for a grizzly to become a sheep killer."

"There's lots of other places for sheep," Cloyd reasoned, "but nowhere for grizzlies. And the grizzlies were here before the sheep, no one even knows how long."

With a wink, the Tlingit woman suggested, "Why don't you walk over to that Sixto Loco's camp and tell him those things?"

Cloyd liked it when she joked with him. He had his answer ready for her. "I'm not the one named Loco."

Ursa laughed and said, "We'll steer wide around him,

just like we hope mother grizzly does. With a name like his, I don't imagine the man gets much company up here."

And so they followed the tracks of the grizzlies over the Continental Divide onto the Pacific side, onto the slopes that were drained by Rock Creek. At the head of the basin, the deep crater of Rock Lake sparkled in the afternoon sun at the foot of towering peaks. Rock Creek poured out of the lake, down through the trees and onto a long, boggy meadow flanked on both sides by timber and rockslides and a parade of peaks.

Cloyd and the grizzly woman sat on the short grasses of the Continental Divide, turned yellow and orange by the frosts, and admired the view. Trading the binoculars back and forth, they found the bears at last. It was the grizzly woman who spotted them as they were sliding down a long snowbank far above the lake. Cloyd was amazed when he had his turn. He looked to Ursa for what she would say.

"I've seen them doing this lots of times in Montana and Wyoming," she said. "Some of the biologists say they do it to cool off. . . ."

"But what do you think?"

"I don't have a very scientific explanation," she said with a laugh. "I think they slide down snowbanks just for the fun of it. I've seen them slide down the same snowbank two, three times in a row. One time in Montana, I saw a grizzly sit down on his haunches and watch an especially spectacular sunset. The bear watched for twenty minutes. As soon as the sun had set, he got up and left. I remember writing in my notebook, 'Try and explain that.' "

Cloyd took his turn with the binoculars, but the bears didn't reappear. The grizzly woman thought they must be grazing or hunting marmots around the shallow meltwater lake that the map showed up there near the peaks.

Training the binoculars on the valley of Rock Creek, Cloyd discovered a white sheepherder tent in the trees below the long meadow. Ursa took it to be the camp of the two game wardens who were also searching for the grizzlies Rusty had reported.

Cloyd exclaimed, "They have no idea how close the bears are!"

"They can't be very serious about their search," Ursa said. "I've heard they have horses. Grizzlies can smell horses a long ways off."

"But my horse was with me last summer when I saw the grizzly. . . ."

"I didn't realize that," Ursa said thoughtfully. Ursa seemed to be thinking hard about this. At last she said, "Maybe he showed himself to you on purpose."

Cloyd told himself, That's what I always thought. But he didn't tell this to the grizzly woman. It was too painful to talk about.

"It's sometimes said that bears even know the time and place of their own death. . . ."

Cloyd wondered if Ursa was somehow talking about the bear he had seen killed.

"Maybe that bear of yours," the grizzly woman said, her eyes full of conviction, "maybe that bear that is dead is your spirit bear, Cloyd, your spirit helper. Wouldn't it be true to say you haven't been the same since you met him?"

"Maybe," Cloyd said. He was remembering his

dream, the one of the night before that he wasn't going to tell her. The bear in his dream wanted his blood, wanted to eat all the meat from his bones. Maybe the bear he dreamed was the same bear he had seen killed.

"You feel bad that he is dead, but you can turn your loss into power to do something good, like the old shamans used to do."

"The medicine men?"

"The Tlingit believed that bears could change their shape to become people or other animals. Many other tribes believed this as well. Some shamans, the People said, could do the same. The shamans dreamed deeper and traveled farther than ordinary people with spirit helpers. Shamans with bears as spirit helpers healed the sick with the knowledge they brought back from the spirit world. Bears have the greatest healing powers in the animal world, and they could bestow those powers on a human being."

"I wish I knew all these things that you know," Cloyd said longingly.

Ursa poked him in the ribs. "I only wish my students back in Montana were half as interested as you are in everything I have to say."

"Tell me more about the shamans and the grizzlies and spirit helpers."

"Well, Tlingit shamans considered the grizzly spirit too powerful to adopt as a spirit helper, but the shamans of some other tribes became bear-dreamers and did take grizzlies as spirit helpers. They wore the skins of grizzlies, painted themselves with bear-paw signs, and wore grizzly claws around their necks. In their medicine bundles they'd have teeth and claws . . . they went around the woods eating the plants that bears eat, they shuffled along like bears, they danced like bears. . . ."

Cloyd remembered that he'd woofed like a bear at the Bear Dance, and his fingers had felt like claws. The memory, along with her words, made the hair stand up on the back of his neck. "How did a person become a shaman?" he asked hesitantly.

"By fasting like the bear does in its den. By enduring hardship like we can't even imagine today, cold and hunger beyond our ability to comprehend. At the extremity between life and death, the shaman met his spirit helper, and if he lived, he was changed by his ordeal and he brought back new powers with which to help the people. He, or she, could see into the spirit world for them. Sometimes women became shamans too."

Cloyd wondered if Ursa was telling him something about herself. After a long and thoughtful silence, he thought it was a question he could ask. "Are you a shaman?" he asked respectfully.

Ursa smiled, amused by the thought. "I withdraw from the world when I go out to study the bears, but a few weeks is about as long as I can last before I go back into town for a hot shower and restaurant food."

And then she laughed. "When they went out like that, shamans didn't come back into town every few weeks for Mexican food. To acquire power, you had to withdraw from the world like a bear going into hibernation. True wisdom couldn't be found around people— shamans didn't study at the university. True wisdom could only be found in a place that was very special to the person or the tribe, far away from the village, out in the solitude. Solitude and suffering opened the pathways of knowledge that are normally closed to human beings, the pathways to the world of things that can't be seen."

"The spirit world," Cloyd said.

"I can tell you a shaman's song," she offered. "It's a grizzly bear song of the Tlingit. The shaman is singing his oneness with the bear:

> *"Whu! Bear!*
> *Whu Whu!*
> *So you say*
> *Whu Whu Whu!*
> *You come.*
> *You're a fine young man*
> *You grizzly bear*
> *You crawl out of your fur.*
> *You come*
> *I say Whu Whu Whu!*
> *I throw grease into the fire.*
> *For you*
> *Grizzly Bear*
> *We are the same person!"*

Cloyd asked her to say it two more times. He learned it, every word. He didn't know why, but it was important that he have every word right. As he followed her down off the Divide toward Rock Lake, he was repeating the words to himself over and over.

He didn't know why the bears were important to him and not some other Ute kid in Ignacio or White Mesa or the group home in Durango. But he would accept it, just as Ursa had accepted it. He, not someone else, had found the bearstone. He was the one that the great bear, the father of those three cubs, had shown himself to. He was the one who had spotted the mother and cubs. His grandmother would say that none of these things were accidents. He only knew that there was something between him and those bears, something deeper than he could explain.

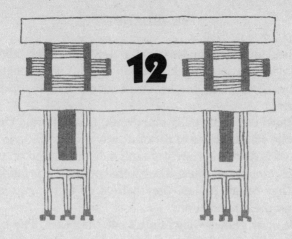

12

In the morning, the grizzly woman was going on her hunches, and she was going fast. Ursa stopped only to glass the cliffs and ledges above. "I don't see our bears on the mountainside," she told Cloyd. "They must have gone up and over. It looks like there's only a couple of routes they could have used."

On top of the "manway," where a foot trail wound up and through a pass considered too rough and rocky for horses, the grizzly woman looked closely for any sign that the bears had passed this way, and found none. Ursa turned the search west, toward a small, U-shaped gap high above them between two sharp peaks. At thirteen thousand feet, the gap towered above the long snowbank where the bears had been sliding.

Cloyd followed Ursa along the ledges as they worked their way through patches of tundra and across scree slides, to the nameless meltwater pond high above the deep crater of Rock Lake. In the soft soil along its shore Ursa found the bear's enormous five-toed print again.

Cloyd fell to his belly and drank, then followed Ursa up the steep incline of rock and ice toward that gap in the sky. At the grizzly woman's side, he inched up the final pitch on all fours. They were both going as quietly as they could. At last they bellied up to the gap and stuck their heads over.

At first glance Cloyd didn't see the bears. The turquoise lake far below, a rectangular jewel nearly the color of a robin's egg, captured all his attention. It was called Lake Mary Alice on the map. Its perch was so high and so forbidding, there wasn't a bit of grass around that lake, only rockflows and boulders and ice. Mary Alice lay in the shade at the foot of Mt. Oso's sheer north face, vaulting fifteen hundred feet above. An ice shelf, glowing blue, clung to the side of the lake at the bottom of the peak. It was a wild place, primitive and beautiful, unlike anything he had seen in all his days of crawling around in the canyons and the mountains.

"Glass the outlet," Ursa said, and handed him the big binoculars.

Cloyd found the tiny stream flowing out of the lake, and there he found his bears. Big as life through the field glasses, the mother grizzly was splashing in the tiny outlet stream. He thought she might be playing, until he saw her pin a fish with her paw, then take it in her teeth. When she dropped it in the rocks, two of the cubs lunged for the trout at the same time, and the brown took it away from the gray-black.

"It's late for spawning," the grizzly woman commented, "but the ice probably hasn't been off this lake very long. In the shade of this mountain the way it sits, the surface of this lake must stay open only a few months out of the year."

Now the grizzly had caught another, and the third cub, the cocoa-colored one, claimed this fish.

The grizzly woman turned to Cloyd with a look of deep satisfaction. "The last grizzlies in Colorado, making a bear living."

Ursa began to take pictures through her long telephoto lens, dozens of pictures. "We won't be able to get any closer than this," she whispered. "If we started over this edge, they'd hear us in a second. Sound would carry in this bowl like anything. But we've got plenty of proof now."

Cloyd whispered, "I don't see how we could get down."

"The map doesn't show any trails, from up here or from down below. Judging by the contour lines, from down on Vallecito Creek it would be a nightmare bushwhack if you tried to climb up into this Roell Creek Basin. It's a perfect refuge for bears."

The gray-black cub was chasing down a fish that was about to flip-flop its way back into the lake. Now a paw pinned the trout to the ground, and the cub took a bite out of it.

By midafternoon, the sun hadn't shone on the lake. Cloyd realized it never would again this year. The sun was too low in the sky, and the peak too high.

The cubs had long since filled their stomachs, but Cloyd could see through the binoculars that their mother was still fishing and still eating. The gray-black cub came over and attempted to nurse, but its mother with a swat sent it tumbling.

When Cloyd told the grizzly woman what he had seen, she said that besides being busy, their mother might be starting to wean them from her milk. "They've come a long way since the end of January," she said. "They're so tiny when they're born—they're hardly bigger than chipmunks. The first month their mother's still snoozing, and they're nursing and growing and sleeping."

The gray-black cub was back at its mother's side, maybe hoping she would change her mind. The brown cub and the cocoa were ambling out of view, over the edge of the lake shelf.

It was an amble that saved their lives.

Cloyd didn't know what was happening, and neither did Ursa. Out of the blue sky, there came a shearing, explosive crack as loud as close lightning. It sounded like trains colliding, it sounded like a mountain splitting in two. Boy and woman looked at each other in shock and in fear for their lives. "Earthquake?" Ursa muttered.

But the mountain underneath them wasn't shaking.

Motion caught Cloyd's eye, some motion high up on Mt. Oso, and he looked to see the leading edge of a titanic waterfall where no waterfall had been before. Carrying enormous blocks of ice, the waterfall was cascading down a fissure in the north face of the peak. Ice and water were tearing rock loose as it all came hurtling down; it was happening so fast that it was hard to take it all in, and it was overwhelmingly loud in this nearly closed bowl of peaks.

The mother grizzly was standing on two legs, trying

to discern the source of the danger. She looked this way and that, and she couldn't tell which way to flee. Her death was raining down on her from above.

Helplessly, Cloyd saw it happen. In a moment the grizzly's life was snuffed out, and the life of her gray-black cub as well.

"Oh my God," cried the grizzly woman.

It took a minute or two for the torrent of water to become a trickle, and several more minutes for the last slides of finest rock to pour into the far side of the lake. Then it was quiet again, all quiet.

"An ice dam must have broken up," Ursa concluded. "In a crevasse up near the peak."

"The cubs!" Cloyd cried. He could see the two sur-vivors through the glasses, coming up over the edge of the lake shelf and looking around for their mother.

It wasn't long before their noses led them to their mother's scent. Through the field glasses, Cloyd could see a small dark patch among the rocks that had to be a bit of her fur showing. The gray-black cub was com-pletely buried.

Cloyd could hear something, some new sound. The high bowl of stone around the lake amplified the sound uncannily. It was the whimpering of the orphans that was coming to his ears.

Cloyd stood up and started to look for the way down. He wanted to get down there to the cubs. The bears had known a way down to the lake. Now he thought he saw it. A ledge angled down through the cliffs and onto the rockslides. "I think we can get down there," he told her, and pointed.

The grizzly woman was shaking her head.

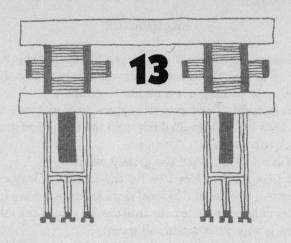

Cloyd couldn't understand why Ursa had insisted they leave the cubs behind like they did. He was confused, and still stunned. All he could think of was those two cubs, so alone and bewildered.

He was following Ursa back down to Rock Lake, where a sheepherder tent, tiny and white from this height, had been erected while they were on the mountain. "But can those two cubs make it on their own?" Cloyd asked doubtfully.

The grizzly woman was picking her way down from the heights in grim silence. "We just have to hope they can," she answered without taking her eyes off the ground. Ursa's voice didn't seem to have much hope at all in it. Then she added, "I can't see a thing we could have done that would do them any good."

It was late in the afternoon. There would be time,

during tomorrow's long walk back to East Ute Creek, to ask the grizzly woman what would happen to those cubs.

As they dropped closer to the lake, they could see two men in gray uniforms fishing down below from the grassy spot where the creek ran out of the lake. "The game wardens who are looking for grizzlies," Ursa said.

"Do you think they heard the mountain cracking and the rocks falling?"

"From down there, I wouldn't think so. That mountain we were watching from is in between."

Cloyd wouldn't have spoken to the two men with starched gray shirts and brass nameplates who were fishing at the lake. He wouldn't have spoken to the gray-haired older man who stood straight as a soldier even when he was fishing. And he wouldn't have spoken to the younger one either, the one with the big smile and curly blond hair who had waved them over.

Cloyd had learned the hard way, the summer before, not to talk about bears that he had seen.

But the grizzly woman was a professor, and she was used to working with men from the fish and game departments in Wyoming and Montana, and she assumed she needed to report finding grizzlies alive in Colorado. Before Cloyd could even think to warn her, Ursa was talking to them and telling them everything.

The younger, whose nameplate said Simpson, was amazed as Ursa told them who she was, of finding the bears, of the proof in her camera. His smile was replaced by surprise and disappointment as the grizzly woman told of the death of the mother grizzly and the gray-black cub.

The older man, Haverford, showed no emotion throughout her telling. But Cloyd could see that he didn't like this Indian woman who was a professor who'd gone looking for grizzlies on her own. Haverford's bristly gray hair made him look like he'd been buzzed by a helicopter flying upside down.

"I specialized in bear biology and behavior," the younger man was saying. "Those two cubs' chances can't be good. There's starvation, predators, accidents," he explained with a glance at Haverford, "and the problem of denning. Those two cubs would be denning with their mother this coming winter."

"Quote me some odds," Haverford said. It was clear who was in charge. Cloyd was afraid of this man. If only he'd been able to think more clearly. If only he had warned Ursa.

Simpson hesitated, then said, "I could be wrong, but I'd give each cub a one-in-five chance of being alive next summer. For both, if I remember my math, one-in-twenty-five."

"Slim odds," Haverford put in disapprovingly.

"What do *you* think?" Simpson asked the grizzly woman.

With a glance at Cloyd, Ursa said, "I'm afraid your odds are . . . realistic. We're going to have to go four-fifths on hope that at least one of them survives. That will keep reintroduction alive, right? More would be brought in?"

Simpson looked at the older game warden almost apologetically and said, "That'd be the way we're all reading the Endangered Species Act, what it would mean in this case. Eventually."

Haverford, who'd said almost nothing, now said

coolly and mechanically, "The Endangered Species Act requires us to protect those two cubs that survived."

Cloyd watched the confusion in the grizzly woman's face and the regret clouding the face of the younger man. "What are you getting at?" the grizzly woman asked with alarm.

"We've got to take the cubs out," Haverford stated, with no emotion at all.

Cloyd felt sick, down deep in the pit of his stomach.

"Oh, no," the grizzly woman said quickly, as she tried to catch Haverford's eyes. "If you take them out, grizzlies will be extinct in the wild in Colorado. You know how it works. The Endangered Species Act won't be applied. There has to be at least one grizzly surviving here to make a clear case for reintroduction."

"That may be the case," the man replied with an indifferent shrug, "but our job is to protect those individual grizzly cubs."

"You can't take them out," Ursa pleaded. The grizzly woman was trapped, and her eyes flashed wildly here and there as she tried to think. Cloyd could see that Ursa knew now, the younger warden knew too, that she had made a big mistake telling Haverford about the cubs. It was the same fatal mistake he had once made.

"They'll wind up in a *zoo*," she pleaded, unbelieving, angry, almost begging. "There's already plenty of grizzlies in zoos, and zoos are no place for them! These are Colorado's last grizzlies you're talking about!"

Cloyd was trying to think. "Can they be raised in a zoo and then be brought back here?"

Simpson shook his head. "No, there's no chance of

that. That would never happen. They'd starve. They would've lost their fear of people—they'd become problem bears. There's no chance of that happening."

"I'm going to try to call Denver," Haverford said. "They'll decide."

"The Division of Wildlife," Simpson explained.

The game wardens were watching the night sky for the last flight from Denver. Cloyd and the grizzly woman had set up their camp nearby. Ursa was muttering to herself, and then Cloyd realized she was talking to him. "Such bad luck! I'm so sorry . . . and I never for a moment considered they might have a ground-to-air radio. I should have suspected."

But Ursa hadn't given up yet. After she and Cloyd ate, she returned to the wardens' campfire.

"Been on it a number of times," Haverford was saying to the younger warden. "Half the time it flies right over Rock Lake. Gets into the Durango airport at 8:40 P.M. It should be over here fifteen minutes shy of that."

Simpson checked his watch. "That'd be ten minutes from now."

Ursa was pacing in front of their fire. "Please," she pleaded. "Think about what you're doing."

"If you don't mind—," Haverford said. He walked a short way down the lakeshore to get away from her. The ground-to-air radio in his hand looked like a black telephone with an antenna.

"I'm sorry," the younger man said to the grizzly woman.

"He doesn't understand," Ursa said. "Have him tell the Division, in all likelihood there are no other grizzlies in Colorado but those two cubs. If you take them out, there will be none left in Colorado."

Simpson rubbed his eyes wearily. "They'll know that, I assure you."

Cloyd was thinking hard. He thought it might be possible to pass close enough to the gray-haired man to grab his radio and toss it way out into the lake.

It would be a crazy thing to do. No, he couldn't do that. All he could do was hope that the plane wouldn't pass over Rock Lake tonight.

"Why doesn't he care?" Ursa was asking Simpson.

The man scratched his chin, and then he bit his lip, but finally he decided to speak. "Please don't quote me on any of this," he said. "You can talk to Tom until you're blue in the face. Before he was with the Division he worked fifteen years as a government trapper. Rifle, trap, and poison are where he's coming from. Tom's from an old Colorado ranching family, and he grew up believing there's good animals and bad animals. With the bad animals out of the way, there's more deer and elk for hunters, and no hazards for sheep and cattle on the public land. He just doesn't understand or appreciate the natural scheme of things."

The grizzly woman sat down on a rock, looking defeated. "A government trapper turned game warden." She sighed.

Now Cloyd could hear the airplane.

The older warden dashed away from the lake, into the clearing beyond the stunted spruces, and began talking into his radio. Cloyd could see the lights of the plane now as it came quickly their way.

"Emergency, emergency!" the game warden was calling. "Tom Haverford, Colorado Division of Wildlife on the ground at Rock Lake. Do you read me?"

"Reading you fine," the radio crackled. "Make it quick. Be by you in a few seconds."

"Division helicopter needed at Rock Lake early to-morrow. Two grizzly bear cubs orphaned and in need of evacuation. Bring hypos with cub dosages."

"Message received," the pilot replied.

Just as the plane passed over the high peaks, Cloyd heard the word "Grizzlies!" crackling on the radio.

Ursa left the fireside and walked into the darkness. Bad luck, Cloyd thought. Such bad, bad luck.

Cloyd found her a while later up on the hillside above the lake. It was cold, and Ursa didn't have her jacket or her wool hat with her. She was crying.

He sat down beside her. He wasn't going to ask her not to cry. He wanted to cry too. All he could say was, "Maybe they won't be that easy to catch. Maybe there's no place to land over there."

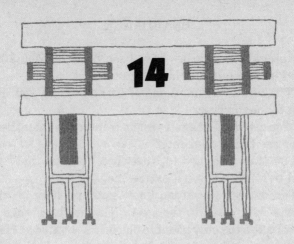

The helicopter arrived midmorning. The pilot who climbed out wore the gray shirt and the insignia of the state wildlife department. The grizzly woman pleaded with this warden too. He had those kind of sunglasses that looked like silver mirrors, and Cloyd could see the Indian woman's round face and delicate chin in those sunglasses. Ursa was shouting to be heard over the roar of the helicopter's motor and whirling blades. "There's no future for grizzlies in Colorado if you take them out!"

"Sorry, ma'am," he told her. "I've checked with the Division in Denver. They say we have to protect these *particular* grizzlies, not the *idea* of grizzlies. That's our responsibility."

"Name me a state," she said desperately, "name me

a state where grizzlies have been brought back after the last one in the wild was gone."

"I'm sorry, ma'am. Some of us agree with you. I'm just following orders."

"You could kill them trying to tranquilize them! Bear cubs are tricky to sedate!"

The man motioned to Haverford. "I know that," he told her. "Now if you'll excuse me. . . ."

The new game warden knew exactly where to land in the wild basin to the west. "The northern edge of Lost Lake's the only possible place," he shouted as Haverford and Simpson started toward the helicopter. "We'll have to get to Lake Mary Alice from there on foot."

Ursa ran for her map as soon as the helicopter had taken off. She and Cloyd spread it out on the ground and studied the wild, narrow canyon of Roell Creek. The creek ran east-west, with a towering ridge high above it on the north side. On the south side of the creek, three lakes were tucked in high bowls with peaks horseshoeing around them.

"Lost Lake sits in between Mary Alice and Hidden, but the peaks cut each off from the other," the grizzly woman observed. "When they land at Lost Lake, they'll have to drop down through the timber to the canyon bottom, then climb all the way up to Mary Alice. These rockslides the last half mile are awful steep. It's going to take them some time to get there. We could watch them from our spot up above."

All the way up the mountain, Cloyd kept hoping that the cubs had fled. But when he and the grizzly woman finally looked down on Lake Mary Alice, the cubs were still there by the high blue lake, still at the side of their dead mother.

"We could shout," Cloyd said. "Scare them away."

"But the only way for them to go is down. There's no cover for another mile down there. We'd only chase the cubs toward those men and save them the climb up the mountain."

The wardens didn't appear, and didn't appear. Cloyd was studying the way down to the lake from this perch in the sky he shared with Ursa. Only the one ledge was difficult, and it didn't look so bad, really. He wished he could go down there. If only there was something he could do.

It was the middle of the afternoon before the three men finally appeared. They were lugging a rifle and two of those fiberglass cages people use to send their dogs on the airplanes.

The cubs scampered away onto the ice shelf, but then they edged back toward their mother. It didn't take long before Haverford's first shot rang out, and then the second. The limp forms of the cubs were loaded into the fiberglass cages, and then the men disappeared with the cubs over the rim of the high lake.

It wasn't a full moon. It was three-quarters of a moon, rising an hour before midnight. But it was bright enough to light Cloyd's way as he slipped out of his tent at Rock Lake. He had a lot of hard climbing to do, and he went quickly, resting only when he had to, watching his heaving breath turn to ice crystals in the freezing night air. He knew the way to the gap. He wouldn't have asked Ursa to come along; he didn't want her to get the blame.

The air was thin and burned his lungs just as badly as before. But at last he was back in the tiny gap between peaks again. Cloyd pulled his wool hat down over his ears. His hands were cold, but blowing on them helped. In the moonlight, Mary Alice shone black and silver instead of blue, and around its north side the snowbanks were shining so brightly they seemed lit up with lights. He guessed it must be half an hour after midnight.

Cloyd started down, picking his way carefully down the ledge. A misstep, he knew, and he'd fall to his death. Yet the bears had come this way, and he could use all fours like a bear. He had those canyon crawling years back in Utah behind him. His hands were like claws, his feet were sure. In two minutes' time the steepest, slanting part was behind him, and he was starting down, slowly picking his way down the uncertain, sliding scree.

Finally he dropped to the lakeside, at the foot of the hovering, treacherous peak of Mt. Oso, and he walked the ice-free shore on the north side toward the outlet. Without pausing to locate the dead bear, he turned his back on the lake and dropped over its rim. As steep and rocky as this slope was, it wasn't nearly so difficult as above the lake. He made good time, and before long he was hastening down the very bottom of the narrow canyon.

Cloyd descended to the elevation of the first tundra and bushes and then headed through the first stunted trees at timberline, toward the shaggy shapes of the spruce forest below.

His map was in the daypack on his back, but he didn't need to pull it out. He knew that the creek coming down in waterfalls from the left, in leaps through the trees, had to be flowing out of Lost Lake up where the helicopter had landed. Cloyd began to climb his way up through a maze of deadfall timber. He only hoped that the grizzly woman was right, that the game wardens would have moved slowly with those cages, returning too late to fly out. They would have had to spend the night at Lost Lake. It would be too dangerous to fly out of the Roell Creek Basin in anything but good light.

Carefully, carefully, he made his way out of the trees at the top of the slope and into the brushy willows. Then he saw the lake, gleaming below its horseshoe of rockflows and snowbanks and jutting peaks. Yes, there was the helicopter near the lakeside, its blades gleaming in the moonlight, in a large grassy opening among clusters of dwarf spruces. Not far away, the men's tent. And not far away from the tent, there were the two white fiberglass cages side by side.

On his elbows and knees, Cloyd crept out of his cover in the bushes. It was a good thing that the men were sleeping in a tent instead of out in the open. He crept closer, pausing to listen. One of the men was snoring. He could see the whites of the cubs' eyes as they looked his way. They could see him coming, but they made no sound.

Before he tried to open the cages, he studied how to do it. Just a little thumb latch beside the barred door.

He only hoped the cubs wouldn't make a sound. Yet, as he took a good look at them, it was apparent they weren't going to. Their eyes seemed so forlorn, so confused and so sad. The muzzles of both cubs, between their soft black noses and their eyes, were almost blond, lighter than the rest of their fur.

One, two, he let them go, and he watched them lope away, the brown and the cocoa. Before they disappeared into the woods, the brown one turned and sat on its haunches a second and looked back at him. "Good luck, bear," he said under his breath. Now the brown cub vanished too, and Cloyd quickly made for the cover of the willow bushes. He had a long and hard way to go before dawn.

Even on his way back down the mountain to the camp at Rock Lake it began to eat at him, what he had done. Yes, the cubs were free, but now what? Somewhere out there in the wild basin of Roell Creek, they were suddenly adrift in a frightening new world without their mother. What if, without her to lead, they were to walk right over a cliff? What if a mountain lion found them? Worse yet, what if they began to slowly, slowly starve to death?

The grizzly woman had thought that leaving them to their chances was the best and only right thing to do, and he had thought so too.

But now he wasn't so sure.

Maybe the grizzly woman was wrong. Maybe he was wrong. At least the cubs would have survived if they'd been taken to a zoo.

The moon had set behind the high peaks as Cloyd was descending the last stretch of the manway down to Rock Lake. But at twelve thousand feet in the thin air, starlight alone was sufficient to light the faint trail if he watched every single step.

The night lingered. The cold had even more bite as

morning finally neared. At last he was off the mountain. Dawn was barely beginning to show as he slipped into his tent and collapsed in his sleeping bag.

As exhausted as he was, Cloyd couldn't sleep. Those two cubs tormented him, especially the memory of their eyes, the whites of their eyes and their forlorn faces.

He wouldn't tell the grizzly woman what he had done. He would wait and see what happened. It was best to be cautious now. As his grandmother always said, "If your mouth isn't open, a bee won't fly into it."

When the helicopter returned at midday with the wardens, they were baffled. Cloyd watched carefully as they told about the cages being open when they awoke, and the bears gone. They didn't suspect him or the grizzly woman. It hadn't crossed their minds that one of them could have crossed the peaks in the night. They thought that the grizzly cubs had reached out through the openings in the doors and undone the latches themselves—they'd heard of raccoons doing the same kind of thing. The wardens had spent all morning looking for the bears.

The grizzly woman didn't even try to mask her feelings. "It's all for the best," she told the two men. "Now let them be."

"I won't promise that," Haverford said gruffly. "There'll have to be an official decision made about it. We still might come back and try to catch them."

Ursa turned to the younger warden. "What do you think about that?"

"Highly unlikely," he replied. "They've flown the coop now, and they're down in the trees where they'd be about impossible to catch."

The older man couldn't conceal his feelings any longer. Haverford turned on the grizzly woman and said, "You don't care about the sheepmen, the cattlemen, and all the hikers, do you?"

Cloyd watched the Tlingit woman's face. Ursa spoke calmly, with great dignity. "Ranchers can be compensated for their losses to grizzlies, and hikers wouldn't stop coming here. A quarter of a million hikers every year visit the backcountry in Yellowstone. . . . People who visit wilderness don't want it to be totally safe— otherwise it wouldn't be wilderness. They learn how to behave in bear country."

Haverford's jaw was set, and he wouldn't listen, but Ursa didn't seem to be talking just to him anymore. Her eyes were serene and radiant. "In grizzly country," she explained, finding Cloyd's eyes, "the water tastes sweeter and the stars shine brighter."

Cloyd was glad he'd opened those cages.

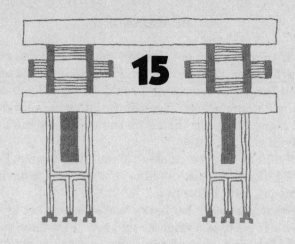

15

Cloyd and the grizzly woman were marching back to East Ute Creek, rarely talking, walking hard, thinking about all that had happened. It was a cloudy day, but the clouds weren't the billowing thunderheads of summer. They had stopped to eat a little dried fruit and trail mix when a front appeared from the southwest like an advancing wave, its clouds high and ribbed at first, but quickly following with darker, thicker clouds and wind that bit like winter.

"Snow tonight?" Cloyd wondered.

"I think you're right," the grizzly woman replied. "Tomorrow's September third. But there'll be Indian summer coming. It'll be a beautiful time in the mountains."

"Those cubs are supposed to be putting on fat now."

"If they can just get through this fall and den successfully, they'll be around for a long, long time. I only wish there was something I could do. I'll tell you one thing for sure, Cloyd. Come June, I'll be back looking for them. I'll give it the entire summer. If we can find one alive . . ."

"I'll help you," he quickly offered. "If you want."

"I'd like that," she told him. "I'm not used to having company, but I'd like that."

She was hoisting her heavy backpack onto her knee, then her shoulders when he told her, "I let those cubs go." He hadn't known he was going to tell her, but now he had.

The grizzly woman's face reflected her astonishment, then her joy.

Cloyd told of his night crossing into the Roell Creek Basin. "Fights for Bears," she said when he was done, and gave him a poke in the ribs. "I knew that was a good name for you!"

The old man had built up the fire, and they could see its beacon through the gathering dusk. Walter Landis had his wool gloves on and he had pulled his wool cap down over his ears. The wind was fanning sparks into the night; the storm was close. The old man's face lit up as Cloyd walked into the clearing, with the grizzly woman right behind him.

Walter Landis was coughing worse than before, and wheezing too as he spoke. "Altitude," he said, "that's all it is. I'll be fine once I get down to the farm."

"Did you find it?" Cloyd had to know. "Did you find one of the caches?"

"Sure didn't," Walter Landis replied almost happily,

and then he fetched four small rock samples out of his jacket pocket. "Actually, I quit on that metal detector and went back to prospecting, the way I first found the Pride of the West. Went looking for a vein."

"Did you find one?"

"Sure didn't," the old man said just as happily as before. "But I found some promising float." He held out four glittering samples, blue-gray minerals bedded in quartz, and Cloyd took them in his hand.

"This is high-grade galena ore, Cloyd. I found these pieces of float this afternoon, on the ridge up above us here, where the mine is supposed to be."

The old man's eyes sparkled with conviction. "My guess is that they've drifted down the slope from the mine entrance itself. From *la Mina Perdida de la Ventana*."

"Maybe we could find the mine tomorrow," Cloyd said.

The old man started coughing. "One day more, and then the morning after that it's time to go home. But now, tell me about the bears. Find any grizzes?"

Cloyd told his story. When he told of the game warden sending for the helicopter, Walter Landis shook his head and said, "The government works in mysterious ways. I saw a grizzly at the Denver Zoo once. It made a sad sight, the grandest animal you'll ever see all fenced in by concrete walls. I'll never forget how clever he was with his claws—just sat there peeling a peach as delicate as you please."

By morning the storm had come and gone, and the day had dawned clear. There were several inches of slushy snow on the tents and on the world of East Ute Creek.

To Cloyd's surprise, Walter Landis announced that he didn't want to spend this day looking for the lost mine. "No," he said, "I've thought about it, and these blue skies are my answer. That mine has eluded discovery for going on two hundred and fifty years now. I might find it, but then again there's at least a chance I might not. I still believe in that legend, Cloyd. Someone, some day, will rediscover the mine and prove the story true. And somewhere in these mountains, there's that room of solid gold I dreamed about my whole life . . . but I have an even better dream today. I'd like to ride up to the Window itself with my Ute guide, if he can arrange it. I haven't even had a peek at it yet!"

Cloyd didn't know what to say. Walter Landis had his heart set on the Window, but the Window was high, maybe too high for him. Cloyd told him so.

"Been looking at it on the map," the old man said. "Twelve thousand eight hundred and fifty-seven feet. I really want to stand in that spot with you, Cloyd."

And so they saddled their horses, Blueboy and the sorrel mare, and they rode up East Ute Creek and onto the Divide, with the Pyramid dominating the sky to the northeast. Everywhere they looked, the new snow lingered on the slopes that lay in the shade.

"How do you feel this morning?" Cloyd asked the old man.

"Full of wrath and cabbage," Walter Landis replied. "Lead on."

Cloyd led the way on the trail that angled high above the timberline across the grassy slope of a mountain that gave them a view down into the headwaters of East Ute Creek. They could see their sheepherder tent

102

there and the grizzly woman's squat mountaineering tent. They could even make out the grizzly woman by the dark braid down her back as she sat on the log by the campfire and made her notes. Ursa had said she wanted to write down everything that had happened in the last week, while she could still remember exactly the way it had happened.

The trail passed through a swale in the Divide, and now they were looking down the Pacific side into the headwaters of the Rincon La Vaca, where the red-haired man had first seen the grizzly and her cubs in May. Cloyd pointed out the broad green meadows of the Pine miles away at the foot of the Rincon La Vaca. "That's the way I came up here last year," he said. "Snowslide Canyon and the Pride of the West are only about five miles down the Pine from that big meadow."

Cloyd saw the Window first, but he said nothing.

A moment later, the old man cried *"La Ventana!"* when he spied the massive notch. As they rode onto the broad, green tundra bench below it, that landmark gap in the long ridge at the Pyramid's shoulder opened wider and wider until they were directly beneath it.

Cloyd could count only one cloud in all the world, and it was clinging to the foot of the San Juan Range so far to the east and south that it was probably down in New Mexico.

The old man's eyes were studying the thread of an elk trail that angled up the slope toward the Window.

"You can't get a horse up there," Cloyd said. "Or at least, you shouldn't. There's no place to turn around."

"Let's leave our horses here by this melt pond."

"You aren't going to try to go up there, are you?"

"Not without your company."

Walter counted the contour lines on the map. "Only five hundred-some foot of climb. That'd be about like climbing the stairs at home fifty times."

Though he was afraid, Cloyd said no more. The old man had his mind made up.

Across the tundra, through the mountain willow, up across the scree slope of fine rock, Cloyd led the way. Walter was limping badly, breathing hard, wheezing, but each time he stopped for a rest he got his breath back, and each time the wide Window looming above pulled him on.

With a hundred yards to go, the old man had a coughing attack that turned his face red, then purple. The coughing wouldn't quit, and Cloyd was scared. Walter motioned for Cloyd's water bottle, and a few sips slowed down the attack. Finally it quit.

"Let's turn back," Cloyd said. "We don't have to get up there."

"Doesn't matter if I fail," Walter replied. "As long as I try my best. I'll be all right now, Cloyd. The spirit is willing. . . ."

Step by step, the old man advanced up the steep slope, and Cloyd followed right behind. They were going to make it after all! At the "Windowsill," he helped Walter up, and then they were both standing in the Window. All the hundred jagged peaks of the Needles and the Grenadiers were spiking into the sky on this new horizon, with the wide Ute Lakes Basin and the three forks of Ute Creek filling up the world in between.

"And here we are," the old man said quietly. "Gosh all fishhooks, what a view."

It seemed so much like a dream, almost like he was dreaming that he had come here with the old man.

It seemed even more like an image from a dream when Walter reached into his pocket and produced the bearstone. It was there on the palm of his hand, that small turquoise grizzly fashioned so long ago by the Ancient Ones. Cloyd didn't know that Walter had brought the bearstone into the mountains.

With his free hand Walter motioned all around him, to the Rio Grande Pyramid, so close and so imposing, to the faraway mesas of New Mexico and Arizona, to the fourteen-thousand-foot peaks of the Needles, to the banded cliffs of the Rio Grande country. "I've been looking for the time and the place to return this," he said, holding up his hand as Cloyd tried to speak. "This is the time, and this is the place."

Cloyd felt the bearstone in his own hand, smooth and blue and powerful, and he felt the old man's hand closing his fingers on it. "I'm much obliged," Walter Landis was saying.

He knew he couldn't refuse the old man this moment, and so he said, "Thank you."

"I won't be back here," the old man said.

With a quick smile, Cloyd said, "You never know for sure."

"No, I know. I'm just lucky I got away with this trip. . . . *You'll* be back here, though. You'll remember this day, whenever you come. You'll remember me."

I *will* come back, Cloyd vowed to himself. "I'll remember," he said.

"Dreams aren't practical things," the old man said quietly. "Not when they first get started. I had a dream of going back to the mountains. . . . It seemed like a crazy idea, but here I am."

Cloyd slipped the bearstone into his pocket. It felt good, having the bearstone in his pocket again. It made him feel strong.

Walter Landis asked, "When did you first dream of coming up here, up this high, where you could look out over it all?"

"That's easy," Cloyd said. "My first day at the farm—it was that day I found the bearstone in the cave way up on the mountain above the farm. I could see a few of the peaks sticking up."

"You can dream, Cloyd. You climbed this mountain here; you must've had to work awful hard to get to the top of that old Rio Grande Pyramid. My gosh, it takes my breath away just looking at it. Your dream now, it's about the bears, isn't it?"

"I want those two cubs to live."

The old man acknowledged Cloyd's determination with a simple nod.

They stayed in the Window a long while, as the sun rode toward the Needles and the Grenadiers. At last they both knew it was time to go.

They were just about to start down when the old man took one last look around. "There's something I always wanted to do," he said. Then he spat down toward East Ute Creek. "That's my contribution to the great Atlantic Ocean," he said with a grin. "And here's my contribution to the great Pacific Ocean," he declared, hawking toward the Rincon La Vaca.

They came off the mountain laughing.

*　　*　　*

It might not have happened if the bearstone weren't in his pocket and the Tlingit grizzly song in his head. The grizzly woman and the old man were both asleep that last night in the camp on East Ute Creek. But Cloyd couldn't sleep, and he found himself wandering away from the embers of the fire into the chill of the night. The moon was just about to rise; meteors were falling every minute, more meteors than he'd ever seen. His heart was full of thankfulness, for the old man, for the grizzly woman, for the mountains.

It was because of the bears that he couldn't sleep.

Softly, barely moving, he began to do the bear dance, forward and back. Where were those cubs tonight? Still alive?

He was the one who had opened their cages. This night they might be starving to death.

He began to chant the Tlingit song the grizzly woman had taught him:

> *"Whu! Bear!*
> *Whu Whu!*
> *So you say*
> *Whu Whu Whu!*
> *You come."*

It came to him as he was singing and dancing, something he could do for those cubs. He had a rod and a reel, and he was good at catching fish. It was something he could do for them that might make a difference.

In the morning, the old man and the grizzly woman heard him out. He would return to the Roell Creek

Basin, and he would try to feed the cubs for a little while. He could leave fish around for them. He had no doubt he could accomplish this.

Walter Landis wasn't speaking. Walter had seen his determination. Now the old man was thinking hard.

"It's not a bad idea," the grizzly woman said with a glance toward the old man. "Those cubs would be wild as the wind, and you couldn't get near them, but their noses would pick up dead fish, that's for certain. But you'd be all alone, Cloyd. It's always risky to be alone in the mountains."

"I know," he said. "I'll be careful, like you."

The old man didn't speak for a long time, until he said finally, "The bearstone's back in your pocket. Dreams aren't practical, but we can't live without them."

Cloyd was saying good-bye to his horse. He was telling Blueboy that it wouldn't be long before they'd be back at the farm together. He told the blue roan that Ursa would ride him out of the mountains, that it would be an honor to carry the grizzly woman out of the mountains.

It was strange waving good-bye as the old man and the grizzly woman led their strings of horses up the meadow toward the Divide. He shouldered the grizzly woman's pack. It was going to be heavy. The riders were both looking back and waving, and now he gave them a stronger wave. He wondered if he was crazy, if he should yell to them and run toward them up the meadow.

But he had dreamed he could do something for

these bears, and he was the one who had turned them loose. No one else was going to try to help. It was up to him.

Cloyd turned and started up into the forest. Inside him, he didn't feel so alone. He was carrying the strength of three people.

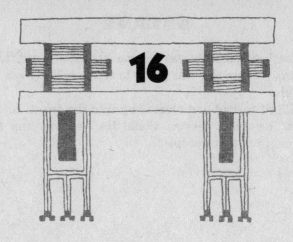

16

Lost Lake deserved its name. Most summers, no hikers
visited Lost Lake. No human beings saw the deer and
the elk come up out of the forest on the shadowy mountainside to graze the short grass around the lake, and
no one saw the occasional mountain goats on the slides
of scree rock across the canyon of Roell Creek. No one
saw the black bears, frequent visitors to this wild basin
where they could feast on the berries that grew thick
along the lush and narrow canyon bottom.

No one saw a Ute boy proceeding slowly down Roell
Creek from above, from somewhere high above. No one
saw how often he stopped to search with his dark eyes
or to sniff the wind. No one heard how silently he
moved as he picked his way through tangles of deadfall
timber up to Lost Lake, and no one heard the splash
of his lure again and again on the surface of the lake,

or the splashing of trout as he brought them to shore.

He gave no shout of excitement, but his heart was singing. These cutthroats were larger and fatter than any he'd caught before. They were all in a frenzy for his little metal spinner on the dome of their world. It was for a good reason they were dying, Cloyd thought, as he was cutting their heads open across their spinal cords to stop their thrashing in the grass. The meat was bright red, and it was firm. These fish were giving up their lives to keep two grizzly cubs and the hope of grizzlies alive.

Were those cubs near enough still to smell these trout? Had they left this basin? Were they even still alive?

On the slope below the lake, in the trees, Cloyd left four fish each at two places a mile from one another. He could only hope that the strong scent of the fish would bring in those bears. The sun had set behind the Needles. He hurried back to his camp at the lake to fix the trout he had saved for himself.

Late the next morning he checked where he had left the fish. At the first place, the trout were gone. He was hopeful, though he couldn't make out tracks. Here he left three more fish.

Still at a distance from the second site, he could hear the magpies squawking. Then he could see those black-and-white pirates at the foot of the boulder field that spilled from the peaks separating Lost Lake and Hidden Lake. He sneaked closer and closer until he had a good view. His four trout were gone. Had the magpies flown off with the fish? It didn't seem likely. Had the cubs come as well? Coyotes maybe? Raccoons?

Next time he wanted to see who was taking his cut-throats. He planted more fish in the dark, then went to see what he could see at first light. He hoped he wasn't too late.

Once again, the first batch was gone.

The magpies were just descending on the second site, the one where the boulder field met the woods. This time he had placed the fish on a spruce that had been felled not so long before by rumbling boulders—its needles were only now beginning to yellow. It was easy to see the silvery fish against that red log.

The birds had jostled two cutthroats to the ground in their commotion, and the third was still in place when he saw a small paw reach for it. Then he saw the blond, doglike face of the brown cub. Brownie! he thought. Now Cocoa's face suddenly appeared. He couldn't quite make out what was wrong, but it looked as if the cocoa cub had sprouted bristles all around the mouth.

Then he knew. Cocoa had learned about porcupines the hard way.

It wasn't but a minute before a black bear appeared, a very large black bear, with its narrow face and a streak of white under its neck. Cloyd was astonished as the bear rushed the cubs and bowled them over with a swipe, growling and baring its fangs.

The cubs scampered away faster than he would have thought possible. With the big black bear in hot pursuit, they fled along the edge of the boulders. The black bear bowled over Cocoa, who was in the rear, and bit hard. Cocoa disappeared, yelping, into the trees as the black bear hesitated, distracted by the squawking of the magpies behind. Then the big bear turned back for the fish.

Cloyd fretted through the afternoon and the evening, but he could come up with no good answers. With that black bear around, he was going to be of no help to the cubs. Over and over, he tried to recall exactly what the cubs had looked like in the morning. They were skinny, too skinny, too weak and too small to defend themselves from animals like that black bear. And Cocoa had a snoutful of porcupine quills. Wouldn't they keep her from eating? Both looked like they were starving.

If only he could talk to the grizzly woman, and ask her what to do. Ursa was probably back in Montana by now. If only she knew he'd found the cubs! If only she could tell him what to do next!

It didn't come to him by thinking. It came to him in a dream, after he'd given up thinking and had given in to his exhaustion. At first he'd thought it was a bad dream. He was back at the Bear Dance, only this time he had fallen in the endurance dance at the very end.

In his dream, all the growler sticks stopped as a result of his fall, and all the dancing stopped. Suddenly a huge bear appeared, motioning toward him with an eagle feather. The bear had an arrow through its neck and one in its heart. He was terrified of this bloody bear, and he couldn't get up. Someone was saying, "It's bad luck to fall. The Bear Dance is over." The growler sticks remained silent, and he glanced over to the big resonating drum. The eight men who'd been chanting and making the thunder were bears also; or were they men who'd sewn the skins of bears closed around them?

He was squinting and trying to tell whether the singers were men or bears when he woke from his dream. He reached for his water bottle. The frightful dream had awakened him. He realized he'd dreamed again of the bear that he had betrayed to Rusty the summer before, the one Rusty had killed, the one the grizzly woman had said might be his spirit helper. He remembered what this bear wanted from him. It wanted his blood and the meat from his bones.

Cloyd drank from his water bottle. Dream-dancing, he thought, raised as much thirst as real dancing. He reached out to the little tent pocket where he kept his tiny flashlight and the bearstone, and he felt for the bearstone in the dark with his fingers.

That's when it came to him, what he could do, what he could try. The singers in his dream had been dressed in the skins of bears. Maybe this was a good dream in disguise.

Hadn't the grizzly woman said that the shamans whose spirit helpers were bears used to wear the skins of bears?

He wasn't a shaman, he knew that. He didn't even have a spirit helper. The grizzly woman had said you could only dream a spirit helper, and the only spirit helper he seemed to dream wanted his life.

He would have to keep going on his own, without a spirit helper.

When Cloyd made his climb he found the big grizzly undisturbed. She was buried in the scree slide, in the shadows beneath the towering north face of Mt. Oso, undisturbed by scavengers or even the spoiling effects of the sun. Working tirelessly, he tore at the scree, throwing the rocks aside until she was free. In the shade of Mt. Oso, the September cold at 12,500 feet had kept her from starting to stink.

All he had was his pocketknife. It would have to be good enough. Fortunately, it was sharp.

He was good at skinning. He had slaughtered many of his grandmother's sheep and goats over the years, and he always fleshed out the hides for her. She tanned them the old way, with the brains, not with battery acid like some people were using.

This skinning was much harder. When the flesh turns cold, it isn't so easy to separate the hide from it. He worked carefully, separating the face of the bear from her skull. Around the paws was the hardest. His knife was dulling terribly. He wished there'd been a whetstone in one of the pockets of the grizzly woman's pack.

But at last, after nearly a day's work, he was done. The cubs' mother looked hideous now, stripped of her fur, a mass of red muscles. His grandmother had told him about this, and now he could see it was true: a bear stripped of its hide looks like a human being.

One last task remained. With his dull knife, he had to sever her skull from her neck bones. He would need the brains.

Covering the grizzly's headless body with rocks, he thanked her for the gift of her skin and skull. The sun was setting as he started down the mountain with the heavy fur over his shoulder and the skull under one arm.

It was going to take time to flesh this hide as best he could, stake it out, then tan it with the brains from

115

the skull. He'd better get started this night. There was no telling how long the cubs would last. Were they males or females? he wondered. One of each?

He would use the biggest of the aluminum pots and mash the brains until they made a paste. Her brains would make just the right amount for tanning her hide. His grandmother had said that it was an example of the fittingness of things: a mouse's brain was just the right amount for tanning a mouse, and the same went for a sheep or a goat.

Or a bear, Cloyd thought.

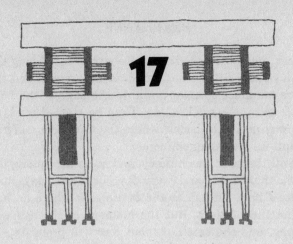

17

With the days growing shorter and the nights longer
and colder, the bears of the Weminuche Wilderness
were heeding the call from within to feed all they
might, to lay in fat against the time of their long sleep.
The big male black bear who counted as part of his
territory the wild and remote basin of Roell Creek was
partial to this high, hanging canyon above all his other
haunts. It was small and confining enough for him to
patrol against other bears, yet large enough to provide
him with more than he could eat during a month's stay
in the fattest time of the year.

The summer's monsoons, sweeping up from Mexico
in July and August, had brought even more rain than
usual to the high country, and more forage than usual.
The black bear was making his rounds, gorging first
on the currants and wild raspberries thick along Roell

Creek, gooseberries and serviceberries too. Along the lush stream bottom he grazed on watercress, and the thick-stemmed grasses flanking the edge of the bogs he found just as delectable. Then he started working his way up the hillsides, where the forest floor offered countless rotting mushrooms.

Still the bear was hungry, and so he kept along the paths that he followed every day. For several days now, there'd been no fish at the two places where he had found them before. But the memory of the fish was strong, and the smell of them was still promising in his memory. He included them in his rounds just in case. At the place by the creek he found no fish, only the lingering smell of fish. Nearing the second place, at the foot of the rockslide, he grew hopeful. The fish smell was strong. But there was another scent too, and it wasn't the human scent he'd first smelled around these fish.

This was bear scent, and it made him irritable. The black bear suspected the cubs that weren't his kind, the grizzly cubs who had appeared in the basin without their mother. He would kill them now if he got the chance.

The fish were there as before, five of them lying on the log, and he began to feed on them, alertly sniffing the wind. The bear scent was still here, still strong. When he was done with the last of the fish, he would look around for those cubs.

As the black bear was starting on the third fish, a big silvertip grizzly appeared suddenly in the boulder field. The grizzly stood to its full height atop a boulder and pawed the air, then woofed threateningly.

Cloyd spread his arms wide and high, showing the

claws that weren't his. What do I do now? he thought. The black bear had dropped the fish in his mouth, but had taken a few steps closer, squinting for a better look and growling. The hairs along its spine were standing on end, and now the black bear was standing on two legs and woofing back at him.

What if he charges me? thought Cloyd. I have nothing to fight with. This is a big bear, this black bear, and he's bristling up for a fight.

"Bears are great bluffers," he remembered Ursa saying, and so he put all his faith in the grizzly woman. If his cubs were to have a chance, he had to run off this black bear.

He's going to charge any second, Cloyd thought. I have to do something first.

Cloyd sprang from the boulder and leaped onto the elk trail at the edge of the boulder field, not thirty feet away from the black bear. From all fours he stood up and made himself tall with his height and his arms. From deep in his throat he brought out a roar that surprised him, hearing it come from inside himself. For a moment he even felt ferocious, growling and displaying his grizzly claws.

The black bear squinted for a better look and saw that this was not only a grizzly, it was one with a human face in addition to its own. The bear turned and ran from the natural superiority of the grizzly and the terrifying oddness of the two faces.

With a look over his shoulder, the black bear glanced back to see the grizzly in pursuit, running on two legs only. The black bear was fast and soon covered the mile down to the lip of the hanging basin where the creek spilled in waterfalls on its plunge to the valley of Vallecito Creek far below. Still in full flight, the black bear picked up the elk trail that led down the mountainside, and in an hour's time was miles away and three thousand feet below.

Two pairs of highly interested eyes and ears had witnessed Cloyd's performance. It was their sense of smell that had brought the cubs to this place. Once again, they had smelled fish. But this time they had also smelled their mother.

They edged closer. The black bear had fled, and the bear that was their mother and yet hadn't sounded or moved like their mother saw them approaching, and took one of the fish in its mouth.

For a long time they watched and waited, and then their hunger and their loneliness drove them close, where their mother's scent was strong and tinged with the suggestion of death.

Cloyd saw them coming in like puppies begging for care yet fearful of a whipping. Their round little ears were forward at one moment, then laid back on their heads the next. Brownie led and Cocoa followed with a muzzle all stuck with quills. Cloyd let them come closer, whimpering. They backed away, came closer yet, backed away again. They were so close now, he could almost reach out and touch them. Their eyes could see he wasn't their mother, yet their noses told them he was. He held out the fish with his claw-covered hand and he began to talk to them soothingly. "C'mon Brownie, c'mon Cocoa. . . ."

Brownie was standing just an arm's length away, swiping at the air with one paw.

"That's right, that's right. . . ."

Cocoa's eyes were forlorn behind the noseful of quills.

Brownie was sitting now, but seemed reluctant to accept the fish from Cloyd's outstretched fingers. Cloyd took the fish again by his teeth, shook it back and forth a few times, then stuck his face out with it toward the little bear's face.

Brownie's eyes and Cloyd's met as slowly, slowly, the cub brought its face close, its dark eyes locked on Cloyd's. The fur on the cub's muzzle was blond, almost gold. Slowly and gingerly, Brownie took the big fish.

Cloyd spent the day with them, right there, with the cubs crawling all over him and mouthing him with their needle-sharp front teeth. Girl bears, he saw, that's what they were. When Brownie broke the skin on his hand once, Cloyd gave her a swat the way her mother would have done and sent her tumbling. After that she didn't bite so hard. Grizzlies had excellent memories, he was discovering. They learned everything fast.

He liked the way they walked flat on their feet, like people. They would stand like little people to play with his hair or to box each other, with one forepaw shielding their faces and the other flailing away. They played with the button on his flannel shirt that was showing between the rawhide boot lacings that brought the bearskin together down his middle. Cocoa let him pry open her mouth; the stub of a quill was lodged in the pink of her jaw. He should pull it, along with the others, before her mouth got infected. His fingers couldn't get a good enough grip, and she bit him. Her back teeth, he noticed, were flat for grinding, like his.

As the sun was dropping behind the Needle Mountains in the west, he began to climb to his camp at Lost

Lake. The cubs followed the bear that almost always walked on two legs, that was not their mother and yet was. At the lake, they sat on their haunches and watched the bear with two faces cast something magical out onto the surface of the lake and bring in fish after fish for them. These fish were alive and needed to be subdued.

Cloyd ate enough of the grizzly woman's trail mix to take the edge off his hunger. Then he crawled in under the low branches on the side of a dwarf spruce thicket away from the wind. The cubs came in and curled up with him. The grizzly's hide would be his sleeping bag this night.

In the morning he would pull the quills from Cocoa's face, and the one inside her mouth, with the tweezers in Ursa's first aid kit.

The trees sheltered him from the wind and the night air, but the cold from the ground was reaching him even through the grizzly's thick fur. Tomorrow he would make a bed of spruce needles under a low-ceilinged overhang he'd seen among the ledges on the steep slope below the lake. Under that roof he'd stay dry if night rains came.

He had to start living like a bear.

The cubs tucked themselves in close as he lay on his side. They had a strong animal smell, like wet dogs, only muskier. His body warmed as it gained heat from the bears. The fast beating of Cocoa's heart slowed as the cub fell asleep, and then it came loud and soothing like the beating of a drum.

The wind rustled the branches of the dwarf spruce, and before long there was thunder crashing over the peaks. It rained, and it rained hard. He should have found a better place to bed down, but if he tried to move the cubs in the storm, he might become separated from them.

The hide was thick, but the rain ran in under the dwarf spruces and found his head, his neck, his legs. The searing white bolts were striking the peaks directly above the lake now, and the thunder was rumbling the ground underneath him. The cubs slept through the storm, but it scared him to be alone and so far away from the farm. What would he do tomorrow, and the next day?

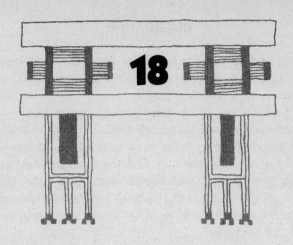

18

Cloyd let Cocoa and Brownie maul him and pummel him and crawl all over him, just as their mother had let them. He talked to them with words and a stream of noises he could make with his lips. The bears learned fast that the skin on his hands was not as tough as his fur-covered body and that he didn't like it if they were too rough with their needle-sharp teeth. Soon they knew his moods and his warnings and his commands from the tone of his voice. They could tell when he was playing and when he wasn't. They couldn't touch his face with tooth or claw, but if he turned sideways, it was a signal he would allow a quick lick with the tongue.

After the first night the three of them sheltered under the rock overhang on the steep, forested slope

below the lake. Besides a good sleeping place, Cloyd
had found a perfect arrowhead there, two inches
long, surely a Ute arrowhead. It was the Weminuche
Utes—his own band—who had hunted in the summers in these mountains. It made him feel good to
know that even the wildest places had been familiar
to them.

Cloyd was marking the days with a tiny notepad and
the stub of a pencil that Ursa had left in her pack. It
was dry under his stone roof during three nights of
hard rains, as the spruces swayed and creaked in the
wind, and the lightning and thunder attacked at in-
tervals all through the night. He was warm in the
grizzly skin on a bed of boughs and needles, and the
two cubs nestled against him added more warmth
still.

Cloyd had made six marks on the notepad, and still
he was reluctant to climb out of their mother's fur. He
didn't want to break the spell. Each day, all day, he
foraged with them. This was the time, while food was
abundant, when they needed to be eating all they could.
Every day was a ceaseless quest for food. He overturned
rotten logs for them and watched approvingly as they
went along licking up the ants and grubs with their
quick tongues. He ate berries alongside them, and watercress along the creek, but he didn't try the mushrooms they relished. They seemed to know which ones
to avoid, but still, the mushrooms were beyond their
prime and swarming with tiny, translucent larvae.

Each morning, a new sheet of clear ice covered Lost
Lake, but the ice would break up by noon. Cloyd kept
fishing for himself and the cubs. He thought about

drying some of the fish, but the sun only appeared above the peaks for three or four hours each day, and the peaks drew clouds. This basin was a cold, cold place, and he began making plans to leave. He wouldn't want to get caught here by a big snow.

It would be up to the cubs whether or not they wanted to follow him out of this basin. It was time for him to be heading back to the old man and the farm on the Piedra. And school, he thought. He hadn't been thinking about it, but school had already started. School seemed as vague and faraway as it had back in the years he used to take his grandmother's sheep and goats out into the canyons. When he got back to school, Mr. Pendleton was going to teach him the secret of making fire with the bow drill.

On the bench by the shore of Lost Lake, he unlaced the bearskin and rolled it into a tight bundle, then tied it off. All the time, he had his eyes on the cubs. They were busy playing hide-and-seek, one of their favorite games. From their mother's skull, he took one of the molars for luck, to go along with the bearstone and the Ute arrowhead. As he was placing their mother's skull in a safe place up in a tree, the cubs were having one of their wrestling and boxing matches, striking each other, dodging, clinching, biting, bristling up and growling in mock battle.

He tied the bundled grizzly skin onto his back-pack.

When the moment came, and he called to the cubs to come along, they showed no surprise that he'd shed his grizzly skin. Everything was the same, nothing was different. He turned to go, and they followed.

For them, Cloyd realized, he was a bear.

They were seeing a bear.

He recalled his grandmother's words from when he was little. In the very earliest time, she'd said, a person could become an animal if he wanted to and an animal could become a person. Sometimes they were animals and sometimes people, and it made no difference.

Climbing into the sky, climbing for that narrow ledge high above the lake of robin's-egg blue that sat at the deadly foot of Mt. Oso, he glanced over his shoulder and saw the two cubs following close behind, the brown and the cocoa. It felt like he was living with these cubs in the very earliest time.

Cloyd led the cubs across the Ute Lakes Basin, but he stayed miles away from the trail. If these cubs were going to have a future, he had to think like their mother.

The meadows down on Middle Ute Creek had turned gold from the frosts. He could see a big patch of white down there, slightly moving. Sixto Loco's big flock. Cloyd could see a long, long way into the Rio Grande country. Below the dark spruce forests, the aspens blanketing the mountainsides were beginning to turn gold.

As he crossed the wide tundra fields, the cubs dug furiously in the runs of countless voles, and succeeded in capturing several. Cloyd was content to chew on his own dwindling food supply.

The cubs were also eating the frosted tops and the roots of certain wildflowers. As they grazed at the edge of a parsnip patch, an almost full-grown family of ptarmigans, more white than brown now with fall advancing, exploded into flight immediately in front of them. Cocoa and Brownie looked at each other in surprise, then gave chase. The cubs put on a burst of speed, but the low-flying ptarmigans were fast, and quickly left them behind.

Cloyd was on his way back to East Ute Creek, to a small food cache that Walter and the grizzly woman had left for him, when he glimpsed a rider far below on the trail bound for the Divide. The man had a string of packhorses behind him. Tony Archuleta, Cloyd realized, on his way home after resupplying Sixto Loco. He recognized Tony's hat, the chaps.

Here was a way to get a message to Walter. He could stay longer with the cubs if he could tell Walter. Cloyd scratched out a note on the little notepad. If he hurried, he could leave the note on the trail for Tony Archuleta to find.

Cloyd told the cubs to stay. He didn't want them near a trail that people used. He sat them down and pushed their noses down and told them to wait there beside his pack.

At first, when he turned away, they started to follow. Once more he told them, and this time he struck each of their muzzles with a sharp tap as he spoke.

This time they did as he said. They watched him go. He realized as he raced away into the forest that it wasn't his doing. It was something their mother had already taught them.

At the place where Cloyd intercepted the trail, he knew he had to work fast. He pegged his note to the center of the trail with a sharp stick. Just to make sure

Tony couldn't miss it, he hastily gathered rocks and shaped them into a large arrow, right in the trail, pointing at the note. Then he fled up the slope, into the trees, to watch.

It wasn't long before Tony Archuleta came along the trail, leading his pack string. Cloyd saw the man with the dark mustache get off his horse, pick up the note, read it, and look all around. But Cloyd wouldn't let himself be seen. Tony smiled broadly as he tucked the note into his shirt pocket, then kicked all the little rocks free of the trail.

Cloyd returned with the cubs to the camp on East Ute Creek and found it quiet and bare, full of good memories. He wouldn't stay long. He only wanted to pick up the food left for him and to cache the heavy bearskin. He might return for it; it made a good blanket. Cloyd removed a long, amber claw from a forepaw to add to the tooth, bearstone, and arrowhead.

He followed the stream down into the aspen forests, where the days were warmer and the nights not as cold. If he could stay with the cubs awhile longer, a week maybe, it would increase their chances. The longer he could stay with them, the better.

As he had guessed, there was still plenty of food lower down. The grass remained green in places, and the cubs found good grazing in the grass and weeds. Brownie and Cocoa slapped at grasshoppers in the air and pounced on the ones on the ground; they even ate moths. Cottontail rabbits were not much trouble for them to catch. They ate the bark from the aspens, they ate rotten mushrooms, they ate willow roots and willow bark. Every day the cubs raked countless chokecherries into their mouths. Cloyd ate just a few. Very many chokecherries would sour his stomach.

The days of mid-September were passing as Cloyd dropped farther still into the tall pine forest, where the cubs robbed squirrels' caches by the dozens. The pine nuts were bigger and oilier than spruce nuts, and Cloyd began to eat them as well, stashing plenty away in his pack. The cubs were amazingly strong. Mostly they were turning over their own rocks and logs now, often working as a team. Their noses led them to the carcass of a deer. Brownie and Cocoa liked that smelly old carcass.

Brownie and Cocoa were thriving. Cloyd could see that they were putting on weight. He thought they might have gained ten or fifteen pounds apiece since he and the grizzly woman had first seen them. What did they weigh now, maybe sixty-five pounds? The fur around their necks and chests was growing extra long and coarse into a ruff, and just behind their necks that trademark hump that grizzlies have above their shoulders was starting to show.

The cubs found acorns plentiful in the scrub oak, and here and there the creek banks were splashed red with wild roses thick with rose hips. Cloyd had chewed on rose hips in the desert, but the fruits of these mountain roses grew fatter and larger and sweeter.

More and more as the days went by, he was grazing alongside the bears, eating the sweet stems of grasses that they ate, trying out the roots they dug up. He swam with them in icy beaver ponds and fished alongside them in the streams. Lying on his belly where the banks overhung the creeks, he practiced at feeling under the banks for trout that hid in the shadows behind dangling roots. He caught four fish that way, one-handed, under the banks.

One day he was sure his hands were feeling the scales of a big fish. It felt a little funny, but he closed on it and pulled it out anyway. Waiting attentively on the bank, Brownie and Cocoa were just as surprised as he was to discover he had a half-grown beaver by the tail. In midair, the beaver was turning around and trying to bite him. Cloyd cried out and threw the beaver up in the air, trying to get it away from him.

The beaver landed on the bank, where the grizzly cubs pounced on it. The beaver was trying to get back into the water, but the cubs knew how to block its escape route. They took turns attacking the beaver, trying for a hold. The beaver stood and faced. Its teeth and claws seemed like formidable weapons to Cloyd, but Cocoa, with a lunge, caught the beaver by the back of its neck. After a few strong shakes, the beaver was dead.

Cloyd kept a piece of the skin and scraped the fur from it. He would soften the skin and sew it into a small pouch with the big needle in the grizzly woman's sewing kit, then hang it from his neck by a rawhide bootlace. In this medicine bundle he would keep the grizzly claw, the grizzly tooth, the arrowhead, and the bearstone.

One day Cloyd was surprised to see Cocoa snap her jaws shut on a bee buzzing by at high speed. With a gulp, she'd swallowed the bee. There were other bees close by, honeybees, and the cubs were curious. They soon discovered a cottonwood with a hive in the cavity where a big branch had broken out. The only trouble was, the bees' nest was about six feet off the ground.

Cloyd wondered how his bears might get at that hive. All he could think of was to offer himself as a ladder. He stood a couple feet away from the tree, then leaned against it. The cubs were quick thinkers. Brownie ran right up his back, with Cocoa barely behind. One stood on his head, one on his shoulder. There was much commotion up there, with all the stirred-up bees and the excited whining of the cubs as they jockeyed for position on his head and shoulders.

Cloyd was stung once on his hand and once on his arm, but he gritted his teeth and held on. With a glance up, he saw Brownie fish out a big piece of honeycomb, and he saw both cubs chewing on the sticky stuff, swallowing honeycomb and bees and all.

He would have liked to stay longer in the lower country. He was keeping track in the grizzly woman's notepad: it was September the 19th, as close as he could tell, the day the cubs came rushing to him, terrified, and froze behind his legs. His instincts weren't as good as theirs. Instead of retreating, he advanced, wondering what had spooked them. Cloyd, and then the cubs too, looked down the slope. He saw a man stalking in a crouch, wearing camouflage clothes and holding a huge compound bow at the ready, the kind Rusty had used. "What the hell," the man swore under his breath when he saw Cloyd and the two cubs at his side.

Cloyd fled, just as terrified as the cubs. He ran as fast as he could. The man chased for a while, and then he quit.

Afterward, Cloyd thought some good had come from this. The cubs had seen a human being, and they had been terrified. Their mother had taught them well. This was good. They would live a lot longer this way.

Cloyd had roamed far from East Ute Creek, up and down the flanks of the mountains above the Rio Grande. Now he started to make his way back to the high country, where it would be safer. At his back he heard the guns of autumn. It was a good lesson for the bears to be fleeing those sounds. He would have to avoid anywhere men could reach on horseback, anywhere hunters might reach from their camps on foot.

Up the steep slopes he led the cubs toward East Ute Creek, through the deadfall timber and across the rockslides and the grassy avalanche chutes. East Ute Creek, where he had said good-bye to Walter and Ursa, seemed like the closest thing to home. But when he was almost back to the old campsite, watching the meadow from the forested slopes above, a party of hunters came riding up the trail, right up the meadows of East Ute Creek. Brownie and Cocoa froze in place and watched the riders pass by far below. Cloyd wished he could stay on East Ute Creek again and fish the stream with his rod and reel. But he would have to lead the bears to safer places.

When the meadow was clear again, he crossed the creek and disappeared with the bears into the timber, heading for the back side of the ridge where there were no trails.

He should've stopped for the night earlier, but it was all steep slopes, nothing that looked hospitable. It was dusk. Then, with no warning, Brownie was gone. The earth had swallowed her up. One second she was investigating some small hole on the slope, the next she was gone.

He should have held on to Cocoa: the two of them were thick as thieves. Now Cocoa was gone down the hole too.

His tiny flashlight with its nearly dead batteries couldn't penetrate the blackness. But he could hear them whimpering, far below.

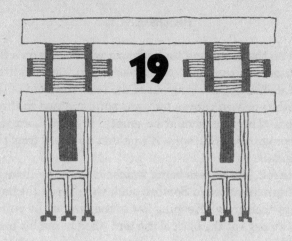

19

He'd taken great pains to skirt the flock and the six sheepdogs guarding the flock.

Where was Sixto Loco?

Cloyd had to get a rope. Only a long rope could possibly save those cubs. He didn't know exactly what he was going to do with it, but he knew he might have to try to squeeze down that hole.

The shadows were growing long, and the flock was moving gradually down the meadow of Middle Ute Creek, headed by habit back to its bedding grounds by the camp.

He could see no movement in the shepherd's camp by the creek. Where was Sixto Loco?

Cloyd watched from the trees as long as he could. Finally he crept in close to the fire. There was a covered pail on the coals, and the coffeepot was sitting on a flat rock next to the coals. No smoke issued from the little metal chimney sticking out of the tent; the front of the weather-beaten canvas tent was shut and tied in three places. The tent should be empty. If Sixto Loco was sleeping inside that tent, it wouldn't be closed from the outside.

He felt like he was being watched. Even the thought of this man called *la Sombra* made the skin on the back of his neck crawl. Keeping low to the ground, he pulled up two pegs at the back of the tent, then poked his head inside.

The floor was covered with woolly sheepskins. A rifle stood in a front corner against a tall pair of snow-shoes. At least Sixto Loco couldn't shoot him with his rifle. Behind the little sheepherder stove, on top of some bags of rock salt, there was the coil of rope he needed. . . .

As he was about to shimmy forward for the rope, he found himself shooting backward on his belly. Some-thing had him by the foot and was dragging him outside.

Cloyd flipped himself over and found the spidery form of the grizzled sheepherder standing over him, the proud *pastor,* the last of the sheepherders of the San Juan Mountains. Somehow the man had slipped a noose over Cloyd's foot without Cloyd even feeling it.

Cloyd's heart jumped. The man looked like an old billy goat, and he seemed to breathe fire.

The eyes were reddened and bloodshot, and they gave the sheepherder a fearful look. Dark and lined and leathery, his face showed no hint of mercy. The gray-black beard grew long and unkempt, like Spanish moss from a tree.

Sixto Archuleta might have been close to seventy years old, but his weathering made it impossible to tell. He could have been younger. His plaid shirt was patched in several places. His waist was wrapped with a curious, braided sash attached to a worn piece of leather. On his hip the man wore a bone-handled knife, and there was a blood smear on his jeans.

In a hesitating tone, low and broken as if the man were unused to speech, Sixto Loco said two words in Spanish: *"Yuta coyote."*

Cloyd was too stunned by the man's appearance, too afraid to speak.

"I caught the Yuta coyote," Sixto Archuleta repeated, this time in accented English, with the trace of a smile crossing his broken, yellowed teeth. The man bent down and undid the noose from Cloyd's ankle.

"Can you talk? You hungry? Don't just sit there! Throw some wood on the fire!"

Cloyd got up cautiously and then did what the man said. He started breaking branches from the pile near the fire. He was looking for the best line if he chose to run. "Sheepmen hate grizzlies," Ursa had said. "Don't let Sixto see your picks and shovels," Tony Archuleta had warned.

As Sixto Loco was adding grounds and water to the big black coffeepot, he asked with a trace of a grin, "Did that old man you were with find any gold?"

Cloyd blew on the coals and determined they were still alive. He was slow to answer as he began to lay wood on the fire. "A nugget in the creek," he answered guardedly.

"My nephew was right about you, Cloyd Atcitty. You're a coyote, a Ute coyote. I see you coming and going around these mountains like a shadow yourself."

What did Sixto Loco know? Cloyd wondered. Did he know about the bears?

The shepherd grinned, showing his broken teeth. His shaggy eyebrows, silver and black, rose as he asked a question. "You and Walter Landis were trying to find *la Mina Perdida de la Ventana,* no?"

"Walter would've liked to find it," Cloyd said truthfully, "but he didn't."

Cloyd could hear bells now, the bells on the goats that were on the leading edge of the big sheep flock. They were returning to their bedding grounds.

Sixto had melted two spoonfuls of lard. The man was always in motion. From inside his tent he brought out a sack of flour, and he rolled the edges of the sack down far enough to expose the flour. Into the sack he poured the melted lard and a cup of water. Cloyd couldn't tell what he was doing. "What about you?" Sixto asked gruffly. "You didn't want to find the mine?"

"I don't like mines," Cloyd said. "I worked in Walter's mine last summer in Snowslide Canyon. It's dark in there, freezing cold. . . ."

"How come you stayed up here by yourself? Are you crazy?"

"I . . . I like it up here."

Cloyd began to hope that he could borrow the rope, as long as he made no mention of the bears. He had to think of an excuse for why he needed it.

138

Cloyd could see that those baleful eyes didn't believe his reason for staying on in the high country alone. The old shepherd pointed with a gnarled finger up above them to the west. "See where the sun's going down on that ridge, right behind the big tree? Yesterday it set in that little notch between that big tree and the dead one. From this campsite, the sun sets right there on a special day. Yesterday was exactly halfway between the longest day and the shortest day of the year. You know what that means, Coyote? Up here, winter's coming soon. I have to take the sheep down pretty quick. After this, you have to be crazier than me to stay up here."

All the while, the spidery man was at work, yet he never seemed hurried. Sixto had five little cakes like thick tortillas frying in the skillet. *"Gordas,"* he said gruffly, pointing with his lips as his hands flattened out five more. " 'Fat ones.' "

The flock had drawn close. It was all familiar to Cloyd, the bleating of the sheep from down in their throats, the quicker, higher blats of the goats.

Suddenly three of the sheepdogs appeared as if from nowhere, and they proceeded to sniff Cloyd cautiously, with their long tails slung low on the ground. The dogs were long-haired, of mixed colors, half wild. He could see the hackles rising on their necks and along their backs.

"They smell something on you," Sixto Archuleta observed as he was pulling the big pail off the coals. The bloodshot eyes fell on Cloyd. "Maybe some kind of animal," the crazy man said with a knowing smile.

Cloyd was so taken aback that he said nothing. He wasn't even sure what Sixto Loco had said.

Now the rest of the dogs were coming around and sniffing him. With a harsh word from Sixto, they scattered.

Cloyd's eyes were devouring those fat tortillas. He was about to reach when the shepherd signaled him to wait, and pried the lid off the pail. The delicious aroma of beans and mutton wafted Cloyd's way. Sixto handed him a ladle. "Spread it on the fat ones," he explained.

Two of the goats had come right up to the campfire and were blatting impatiently. Cloyd could see they needed to be milked. Sixto grabbed one nanny goat by the hind leg and started to milk her. "It's been thirty years since I lost a sheep to a bear," he said proudly, and then he watched for Cloyd's reaction.

Cloyd allowed no emotion to show, and the man continued. "I sleep with one eye open, but really it's the dogs. All six of my dogs, I put them on one of these nanny goats before they even opened their eyes. When they're suckled to a nanny, they grow up thinking they're part goat. They love these animals and they take care of them. They watch out for the sheep too, even though they don't respect them, for often the sheep are stupid snivelers."

"I used to have a flock of sheep and goats," Cloyd said. "A small one." He wanted to milk the second goat himself. The man might offer him some milk. He grabbed her by the leg, as Sixto Archuleta had done. The grizzled shepherd handed him the pail.

It had been a long time, but his fingers could remember.

Sixto strained the milk and passed it to Cloyd. It tasted warm and good. "Now let's eat," the shepherd said.

Cloyd had thought all the eating was done. Maybe Sixto could tell he was still hungry. The shepherd picked out a lamb from the flock and slaughtered it exactly the way Cloyd had learned from his grandmother, and he skinned it exactly the same way too. Sixto fried the blood they had caught, and then he made a stew with carrots and onions and potatoes and plenty of meat.

This night wouldn't be like the others, with his stomach aching when he went to sleep.

Even the lamb's head was set to cook in the coals, a delicacy for the morning. Sixto was like an Indian, Cloyd thought, using every part.

It was the man's eyes that made him look so mean, Cloyd thought, all red and bloodshot. The campfire smoke had made his eyes look that way. It wasn't him. It was all the time he'd spent squatting by campfires.

More *gordas* on the skillet. Sixto was throwing scraps of meat to the dogs. "We have a lot of eating to do, Coyote. You don't have any fat on your ribs, I think."

The dogs were back sniffing his legs again, this time four of them. Their snouts were wrinkled with suspicion, and their tails were down on the ground like the tails of coyotes.

To Cloyd's amazement, Sixto said, "They smell those bears on you. Now tell me what happened to my she-bear and the cub that was almost black. Tell me who

141

the woman was who was with you, who was part Indian but not Ute. Tell me how you come to be with those two cubs, and tell me where they are now."

Cloyd couldn't mask his surprise. "You knew about that mother grizzly and you didn't kill her?"

The old shepherd heaved a sigh and said, "I used to see her boyfriend too once in a while, the one that was killed last summer. Why should I kill them? They're old coyotes like me . . . like you. We're the last of the breed."

Cloyd was trying to take this all in.

"When I was young I killed too many bears," Sixto said. "I was a *tonto,* a stupid. Everyone was young and stupid back then, even the old people."

"You've seen grizzlies up here, and never told anybody?"

"There's still a lot of *tontos* out there."

It was starting to get dark. The shepherd put out a flashing beacon where the flock had bedded down, and he filled a hollowed-out log with rock salt. Afterward, by the campfire, Cloyd told his story, from first seeing the cubs to the death of their mother to losing Brownie and Cocoa down a deep hole on that ridge facing Middle Ute Creek.

"Ayeee," Sixto Archuleta whistled, on hearing what had happened to the cubs.

Cloyd could see the dread in the proud shepherd's face. Something had spooked him, and it wasn't the cubs' predicament. At last Sixto said, "This is bad. I know that place. This is really bad."

The shepherd would say no more. Cloyd wondered if Sixto would help after all. He had to get help to those cubs soon.

142

BEARDANCE

Above the Rio Grande Pyramid, clouds were scudding across the crescent moon. "Look at that," Sixto cried, pointing a crooked finger. "The horns of the moon can't hold any water."

"What does that mean?"

"Weather coming."

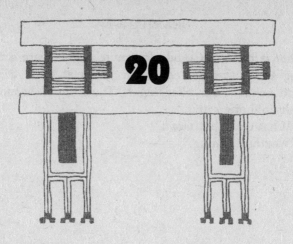

20

Cloyd slept warm with the little sheepherder stove only a few feet away. He hadn't slept so warm since he'd left the farm. In the middle of the night the fire nearly burned out, but Sixto got up and stoked it. The wind was giving the wall tent a bad buffeting, but this tent was so well staked out, it felt strong as a house.

In the morning, the woolly backs of the sheep were covered with an inch or two of snow. The day dawned crisp and clear with five hundred animals all exhaling vapor clouds into the morning air, all huddled close for warmth and protection.

Cloyd was sitting on a log, sharpening his pocket-knife with Sixto's whetstone. There was something about the bears that he'd been thinking about for a long time; Sixto Archuleta might know something about this. "Have you ever seen a grizzly's den? Is it very deep?"

He hoped a den wouldn't be very deep. He didn't know how deep his cubs could dig, or if they would dig a den at all.

" 'Course it's deep," Sixto answered. "I've seen a couple. They tunnel six, eight feet, then make a sleeping room about six feet across. Both of the ones I saw were dug under tree roots. You know what . . . you'd think they'd dig their dens on the slopes facing the sun, where it would be warmer, but they are smart and that would be stupid. They'd be waking up all winter if they did that. The earth keeps them warm enough. They den in the shadows, where the sun won't disturb them until it's spring."

Just then a light plane appeared and buzzed the camp. Its wings were white underneath and red on top. The plane came in so low on the meadow that Cloyd could almost see the pilot. All of a sudden, the sheep were running, scattering, bleating hysterically. Lambs were getting separated from their mothers. It was hard to tell if the lambs or the ewes were more panicked.

Sixto Archuleta's eyes were on fire. Cloyd found out about the narrow sash around the shepherd's waist: after the airplane's second pass, Sixto started picking up stones, and he unleashed the sash from his waist and fitted a stone to it. A sling! Whirling the weapon around and around, Sixto was ready when the plane came back the third time, and he let the stone fly with terrific velocity.

The pilot must have wanted an especially good look, because he was flying even lower than before. The sheep were running recklessly in all directions.

Cloyd couldn't follow the flight of the stone, but he saw the plane coming right toward them, and he saw its windshield suddenly spiderweb all over with cracks as the stone struck.

The boy turned with awe to the shepherd. "Was that a lucky shot?"

Sixto gave him a broken-toothed smile. "I've had a lot of time to practice."

The old sheepherder was satisfied that he had traded trouble for trouble. "That ought to teach them some respect," he said with a grin. Sixto made a circling motion for the dogs with his right hand, and they sprinted off to gather the flock. Sixto did his part too, keeping the sling whirring as he headed off sheep with stones placed barely in front of them.

"What was that guy doing?" Cloyd asked, as finally the two of them set out after the cubs with rope, a flashlight, and a gas lantern.

Sixto shrugged. "Asking for trouble, was all I could see."

Three hours brought them to the place where the cubs had fallen into the earth. The flashlight revealed a nearly vertical slope angling sharply down and away from the opening. There was no way to determine what was below. They listened for the cubs, but could hear nothing. Cloyd called to them with the smacking of the lips they knew, and he called with their names. Then he heard them whimpering, both of them.

"They're alive," he said to Sixto.

"Yes, but it sounds like they're a good way down in there. No way to get them out from here. If you went in there, you might go right over a drop-off."

"Those are the last grizzly bears in Colorado! It's a mine shaft, isn't it?"

The shepherd's eyes were greatly troubled. "For you," he said, "I will tell what I think happened to them. Yes, they've fallen into an old mine."

"This? This is *la Mina Perdida de la Ventana*?"

With a grimace, Sixto said, "I don't know for sure. But I think it is. It's not the entrance. It's a place where they must have been working up from below, following a vein of gold or something. Or else they made it to bring air into the mine; I don't know."

"There's another entrance? You know the main entrance?"

"This mine is an evil place." The old sheepherder's voice was full of hurt. "Dangerous too. You'd go in there after those bears?"

Cloyd remembered how much he feared being inside a mountain. But he answered, as much to himself as to the shepherd, "I have to. I've kept them alive this far."

"Forty-five years ago," Sixto said softly, "my brother died in there. Inside that mine is where he's buried."

Hurt was welling in the shepherd's tired eyes. "I've heard that people say I killed my brother . . . I've lived with that. With his last words, he made me promise two things: to close the mine, and never to go in there again. I have honored my promise."

"What were you doing in there?"

"Digging, what you think? We were just starting to dig. . . ."

"I won't do any digging," Cloyd promised. "I won't even touch the walls. I won't ever tell anyone that I know about this mine. I'll keep your secret. Just show me how to get in there. I have to try."

"I will show you," Sixto said, and then his eyes flashed red and angry. "What about after I'm dead? You'll tell, *tontos* will come to open up the mine. . . ."

"I can keep a secret," Cloyd said, and he meant it.

"Good," Sixto said. "I trust you. But let me tell you something. . . .You believe in ghosts?"

"Maybe . . ." Cloyd admitted. He didn't even want to talk about ghosts.

"Good. I wouldn't be the kind of ghost you would want to have angry with you, Coyote."

The shepherd led him around the ridge and onto a high ledge, until the Window loomed into view. "*La Ventana* on a good day," Sixto reflected as they stopped to catch their breaths. "*El Portal del Diablo* on a bad one."

"*La Ventana* today," Cloyd said uncertainly. He was filled with dread.

Sixto's tired eyes weren't sure either. He was eyeing the fast-moving clouds above the Window and the Pyramid, and he didn't seem to like the look of them. He disappeared behind a leaning slab of rock, and then Cloyd found him there removing a stone the shape of an axe-head from the wall. "This is it," Sixto said. "We'll open it up and set these rocks aside.

Afterward I will seal it up again just as good as you see now."

They'd soon exposed the opening, no more than three feet across and six feet high. Cloyd called for the bears, again and again, but no sound came from the mine except the trickling of water. Sixto lit the lantern. Cloyd had to go now, before he lost his nerve.

Sixto told him, "I'll go back to the other side of the ridge, to where the bears are, and I'll shout down that hole every two or three minutes. Maybe that will help you find where they are. *Vaya con Dios,* my Yuta amigo."

With the coil of rope over his head and across his chest, the lantern in one hand and the flashlight in his back pocket, Cloyd started into the Lost Mine of the Window. Down a short slope and barely into the tunnel beyond, his light fell on two gleaming skulls, their empty eye sockets looking right at him. Cloyd swallowed hard and walked closer. Two skeletons lay side by side, unburied from head to toe. A closer look revealed ancient arrows lying among the rib bones. Ute arrows, he realized. A quick movement startled him. His light caught a bushy-tailed wood rat scurrying into the darkness.

The arrows brought to mind that story in Walter's book, *Lost Mines and Treasures of the San Juan Mountains of Colorado*. This was the part of the story he'd read over and over again. Someone, he remembered, had discovered these two skeletons and had fled, never to return. Sixto and his brother should have run away too, Cloyd thought. I should run away.

Walter Landis, Cloyd realized, would be amazed to

learn that the story in his book was true—but Walter would never know.

Step by step, he moved cautiously forward. The logs supporting the ceiling of the tunnel looked soft and spongy. Walter had always said that old mines with timberwork could cave in if you even looked crossways at them. Cloyd held his breath and kept going. If he lost his nerve . . . It was cold inside the mountain, not much above freezing, and the lantern gave off only a murky light. Following the tunnel's twists and turns, he had to duck low in places.

The ceiling was unsupported by timbers now. He knew that an all-rock tunnel was supposed to be safer, but he didn't feel any safer. His breath came in short gulps. The mountain was squeezing the air out of him.

The ceiling bristled with sharp rocks. At the end of a long straightaway, at a low turn, his head struck the ceiling. Suddenly dirt and rocks were showering down on him. His heart jumped; he expected the worst. He thought for sure he'd brought the mountain down on himself, but he was surprised to find, through the swirling, dusty light, that the roof had held. After a few moments, dead silence returned to the mine. He could quit holding his breath. Now he realized how badly his head hurt. Touching two fingers to the place on the top of his scalp, he brought them back to the light and saw the bright red of his blood.

After a few minutes the pain dulled. Cloyd went on, but his fear was walking way out in front of him. A side tunnel led to a wide room, littered with boulders, that in turn led to an incline too steep to walk safely down. A twenty-foot ladder joined this level to the one below. He tested the first rung of the ladder with his foot. It crumbled with only a little pressure.

Cloyd returned to the main tunnel, but it soon played out. The only way to continue was down the twenty-foot ladder. He went back and stood above the drop a long time, paralyzed. His throat felt like it was stuffed with wool. His fright had a smell to it, an ominous sour smell suddenly coming out of his skin. He turned and fled.

Outside the mine, clouds had covered up the Window. The wind was blowing hard and cold. Winter was on its way. He told himself it was okay to give up. It was time to start back for the farm.

No matter which way he turned it over in his mind, he just couldn't. He couldn't leave the bears behind. He hated that mine and he could sense his own death, but the bears were still inside it, lost in the pitch dark. He'd gone down ropes before, he told himself; he'd climbed up ropes. He had to try.

Cloyd turned and started inside again. This time when he came to the drop and the ladder, he didn't hesitate. Tying off the rope to a boulder, he eased the lantern to the bottom of the drop. With the rope passed behind his back, he started down the slope, bracing with his feet. Toward the bottom he slipped and came down hard. In a heartbeat, the mine was filled with the sound of breaking glass and with utter darkness.

Panicky, he reached for the flashlight and flicked it on. Its light seemed strong enough, but its beam was flickering. These batteries were playing out.

151

How long would they last? His heart gradually stopped racing. He told himself to try to stay calm. The beam would hold for a while. He was going to keep going. Nothing could stop him now unless he was buried with rock.

Farther and farther into the mountain he continued, passing side tunnels that went nowhere. One was closed by a cave-in. He wondered if this was the place where Sixto's brother had met his death.

For a long time, he waded through water halfway to his knees. He was shaking with cold. Water was dripping out of the ceilings and running down the walls. He knew that if he touched anything here, it all might come down.

After Cloyd passed through a series of rooms, the tunnel began to climb. He stopped every few minutes to listen for the bears or for Sixto, but there was no sound but the dripping of water. The tunnel narrowed and climbed. He eased on all fours through an opening braced by rotten timbers. More rooms, more side tunnels that led nowhere, nothing anymore that he could call the main tunnel. The one he was following spoked off into three directions, each leading into rooms where ore had been removed, each climbing and narrowing.

The second tunnel led to a room where the flashlight's beam, flickering from strong to weak and back, fell on another skeleton. His heart jumped in his chest, yet he crept closer. A rusted sword lay close by the bones. Next to the sword lay a rawhide bag chewed apart by rats. He knelt to discover . . . gold coins, perhaps fifty pieces of Spanish gold, each a little bigger than a quarter. Had no one discovered this place before, not even Sixto and his brother?

He would take only one of the coins. . . .

Cloyd backtracked to the third tunnel. A hundred feet into it, he heard something. Not the bears, not the whimpering of the cubs. He listened again. It was Sixto Loco calling, *"Coy-o-te! Yu-ta coy-o-te!"*

He kept moving forward; the echoing voice stopped. Several minutes later Sixto called again, and this time his voice was much stronger. Cloyd yelled back, "Here I am, Sixto, here I am! Where are you, Brownie? Cocoa, hey Cocoa! I'm coming for you!" He made the smacking noise with his lips that he'd used so often to talk to them.

In less than a minute the bears appeared in the shadows at the edge of the light. Then they raced toward him. He got down on the floor of the tunnel with them, and he let them whimper and whine and lick his face and claw him up and down in their excitement.

"Sixto!" he called. "Can you hear me?"

The old sheepherder replied joyously, "I can hear you! I can hear you!"

"They're okay, they're fine. When I come out, though, we can't be around people. I don't want them to be around people."

There was silence, and then Sixto's voice came again. "I understand. You turn them loose, Coyote, then come back to my camp. We'll come out of the mountains together. It's time to come out of the mountains."

Cloyd didn't respond. He hadn't been making plans,

he'd only been going from day to day. There was so much he had to think about.

"What is it?" the shepherd called.

"I'm . . . I'm not sure I can," Cloyd said tentatively. "I might have to stay with them."

"How long?" Sixto called.

"I don't know . . . until I think they're safe."

"You're crazy! Bad weather's coming. It's too high up here, too cold! You might stay a little while, but if you stay too long . . ."

"I'll just stay a little while."

"I tell you what, Coyote, I'll leave my tent right where it is. It's a strong tent. It can stand there all winter I bet. I'll leave the food I've got left. I'll leave the stove, I'll leave some other stuff. I have a pair of snowshoes, and a pair of winter boots. You'll need those things if a big snow comes!"

"Thank you," he called. "Thank you!"

At the place where Cloyd was standing, a side room bulged from a narrow opening in the tunnel. His light followed one of the bears inside, and at first he doubted his eyes. He shone the light all around. There was nothing wrong with his eyes. This was the room, at the end of the Spaniards' tunneling, that Walter Landis had dreamed of his whole life. A natural pocket, its walls were made of gleaming, crystalline gold. This was the freak of nature, the chamber of solid gold that Walter liked to paint with word pictures down on the farm. "The heart of the mountain," Walter called it.

The Spanish hadn't removed this gold when the end came. They'd only just discovered this room.

But he would never tell the old man that he'd been in this mine. And not because of any ghosts. Because Sixto Loco had helped him, and Sixto had asked him to keep a promise.

He turned with the cubs for daylight. When they got to the ledge and the open air, it was snowing.

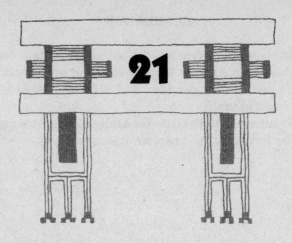

21

Far below, the aspen forest was turning quickly toward its prime. The bears were watching with him. Several days before September ran out, the colors reached their vivid peak, and the flanks of the mountains were all wrapped in blankets of gold sprinkled here and there with patches red like fire.

No wind was arriving to shake the leaves prematurely from the trees. Skies of the deepest blue marked each day as fall hung suspended in its glory. It almost seemed this was the way it always was in the mountains, as if the lightning bolts and the thunder, the drenching rains, the sudden hailstorms, and the early snows were made-up memories.

Sixto Archuleta and his flock had disappeared over the Divide, and the sheepherder too, like the grizzly woman and the old man, had become a memory.

Cloyd was glad he had stayed to see all this, to see it from up high looking down. In the shadows behind the peaks, the new snow lingered. Everywhere else it had burned off. The cubs weren't finding their table as crowded as before. They were depending more and more on roots and nuts. Their claws had grown longer and they'd become more powerful diggers since he first spied them.

Every day Brownie and Cocoa would catch a few mice scurrying between runs in the grass. With a thrown stick, Cloyd struck a grouse that had flown to a low branch. And the cubs smelled out a big beaver that had felled a tree on itself.

A few days after Sixto's flock disappeared over the Divide, Cloyd started for the shepherd's camp on Middle Ute Creek. The ammonia smell of sheep urine was still strong on the meadow. He wanted the bears to continue to avoid the scent of sheep, as their mother had taught them. In the deep timber high above the meadow, he spoke to them and knocked his finger sharply across their muzzles. He told them to stay behind and wait for him.

The sheepherder who was supposed to be so fierce had left his tent pitched for Cloyd, as he had said he would. Inside, Cloyd found all manner of gear that might be useful to him. The first thing Cloyd noticed was the shepherd's sling, which he had worn around his waist, and a note on it that said, *"Bienvenidos, Yuta coyote. The sling is yours. You could be a good shot too if you practiced. Eat the food, use what you like, 'Mi casa es su casa.'* Good luck with your purpose."

The flashlight remained, the axe, the snowboots Sixto had talked about, the long snowshoes with wood frames and rawhide webbing, a big box of matches, the whetstone, lard cans for cooking, two blankets, even the sheepskins on the floor. Most important of all, Sixto had left food strung in a tree. Cloyd lowered the food down and inventoried it. He'd never guessed Sixto would leave this much for him. The sack of flour was here, with the baking powder and salt already mixed in. He could make all the "fat ones" he wanted. Sixto had left cornmeal too, lard, a sack of beans, coffee, even sugar. Cloyd counted four dozen assorted canned goods, including tuna, chicken, pork, peaches, plums, cherries.

He packed all he could carry. Cloyd worked quickly, wanting to return to the bears as soon as he could. He had room for only half the food. He tucked the whetstone into his pack and tied on the big snowboots. When he'd lashed the long snowshoes to the pack, he was done.

It was several days later, as Cloyd was bringing the cubs across the Divide, over the grassy slopes high above the tree line, that he heard the plane. He was heading for the drainages of the Pine River that felt like home and would eventually lead him back to Walter Landis. He'd always hurried the cubs to cover when planes approached, but this time there was nowhere to hide. Cloyd began to run, with his heavy pack bouncing from side to side on his back. It was much heavier than it used to be. The cubs could have run much faster if he wasn't holding them back.

The plane passed over the Divide, a thousand feet above him perhaps. He hoped wildly that the pilot hadn't been looking his way. Now he realized that he should have searched out a rugged spot to cross the Divide, one with plenty of hiding places. At any rate, he shouldn't have run. He should have frozen, made a tent of himself and the leaning backpack that he could have hidden the cubs under.

Too late now. The plane banked and returned, this time flying low. Cloyd huddled with the bears next to a rock sticking out of the tundra, but it was no use. The damage was done. It was that same plane, white under the wings, red on top, only with a new windshield. It buzzed him so closely that he even got a glimpse of the pilot, in a gray shirt, with hair that looked like it had been cut by a helicopter flying upside down.

What did it matter? Cloyd kept telling himself. They couldn't catch him and take the cubs. Now he was down in the timber, now he was on his guard.

Every day the game warden came looking, buzzing all around the mountains like an angry insect. For six days Cloyd kept on the move, visiting basins high above the Pine River that had no trails up them. The Dog Rincon. The Grouse Rincon. Basins with no names. At last he'd come to a deep pond at the head of the rugged Cañon Paso, where he felt secure. The pond hadn't completely iced over yet, and he was catching fish out of it.

The leaves were off the aspens now, blown off by two days of high winds. The first week of October was ending, and the skies were turning gray. He was wearing many layers of clothes now, even his wool gloves and his wool cap in the daytime. Sixto Archuleta's snowboots, rubber on the outside with leather uppers, insulating felt on the inside, were keeping his feet warm and dry. And he had the snowshoes in case he would need them.

There was cover at one edge of the pond, a dense spruce forest. No trail led up the Cañon Paso toward him; there was only the kind of hard going that he and the bears had managed as they sought out the most rugged and protected places. That game warden, Haverford, would never find him. It made his heart go fast—being hunted, being an outlaw. It made him feel like a grizzly himself.

Every day he was practicing with the sling. One time out of six he could hit a piece of granite no bigger than a basketball, across the pond.

He would have felt better if he hadn't lost the bearstone. It happened when they'd first come to this pond. He'd been showing the bearstone to the cubs, telling them about it. Brownie's tongue had quickly flashed, and she'd swallowed the bearstone right before his eyes.

He hoped losing the bearstone wasn't a bad sign. He still hoped he could find the bearstone in one of Brownie's scats.

Maybe the game warden had given up and wasn't hunting him and the bears after all, Cloyd thought. But he knew better. He had a bad feeling.

At least Walter Landis would know by now that he was okay. Walter would have been told about him being spotted by the airplane. Walter would have been told that he was with the cubs, that he was okay.

The old man would be pleased. Walter would like the idea of Cloyd hiding out from that game warden who wanted to bring in the last grizzlies.

By now the game warden must have a pretty good

idea, Cloyd realized, about how those two cubs got out of those cages. It must have made him mad.

It was hard to understand the government. The grizzly woman had said that some of the government people had spent the whole summer trying to find grizzlies in Colorado so they could protect them and bring more. Then there were other government people, like the game warden, who'd like it better if the last grizzly bears were in the zoo.

These cubs were still living wild. He'd been careful not to feed them his food. It was okay for him to graze along with them, but it couldn't work the other way around.

They'd said there wasn't even much chance of one cub surviving. So far they were both doing okay. Why wouldn't the game warden just leave him alone to help them beat the odds?

He hadn't thought that anyone could track him to this place at the head of the Cañon Paso. All the same, he had a bad feeling, and he was keeping sentry now on the bald spot far below.

His fears and his waiting had been justified. Down the mountain, three men were moving across the bald spot. Cloyd recognized the big man in the lead by his bright shock of red hair and the full red beard.

Cloyd's heart was suddenly in his throat. There, right down there, was the man he hated, coming hard and fast after him. Rusty Owens, who'd gone to Alaska. Rusty, the red-haired man, the man who killed the bear. Now Rusty was entering the trees, leading two others up the faint game trail.

Cloyd knew there was only one man who could have

tracked him here—the best hunter, trapper, and tracker in the San Juan Mountains. Rusty wasn't in Alaska any longer.

All the men had snowshoes strapped to their backpacks.

The cubs had seen the men too, or smelled them, and they were just as alarmed as Cloyd.

No need to strike his tent; it was rolled up in his pack. He only kept it for an emergency. He hadn't used it since the day he'd met those cubs and fed them fish and they had followed him up to Lost Lake.

Up and out of the Cañon Paso he climbed, careful to step only on rocks. Brownie and Cocoa seemed to know too. They knew they were being hunted and they seemed to be aware that their tracks would give them away.

Cloyd was determined. *Rusty Owens wouldn't catch him.* He couldn't allow that to happen. Rusty Owens was a proud man. Rusty thought he could do anything. Rusty Owens thought he was the lord of the mountains. But Rusty Owens wouldn't catch him and these cubs.

He climbed up and over, into the basin of the Rincon La Osa, without the men catching sight of him. All the while his lungs were screaming for air. He had climbed more than a thousand feet above the timberline, almost straight up, without ever stopping to slow his heart or catch his breath.

Deeper and deeper into the mountains Cloyd withdrew, zigzagging in a route he judged would be impossible to follow. He kept going through the dusk, finding a place to ball up with the cubs only when he couldn't possibly continue. Before dawn he was up and moving.

Brownie and Cocoa understood his urgency. They often stopped to look and listen. Nothing. If the bears, with their senses, couldn't hear or smell those men . . . He was beginning to feel safe.

Now that he was so close to the Divide, he determined to cross back over to the Rio Grande side. At the head of the Pine River, he skirted the low meadows of Weminuche Pass. In the trees high above the pass, he began to work his way west toward the Ute Creeks by way of the northern slopes of the Rio Grande Pyramid. No trails could be found on that northern side of the Pyramid. It was wild and it was rugged. When it was safe again, he could visit Sixto's camp on Middle Ute Creek and resupply with the food there.

The wind blew hard all night the second night, and the snow began to fall on the third day. Daytime arrived dark and never turned brighter. The snow fell silently hour after hour in flakes big as half-dollars. The wind was gone, it was uncannily quiet. He sheltered with the cubs in a dense cluster of spruce where almost no snow was reaching the ground.

The snow began to fall even more heavily at night. Cloyd had seen snow fall this fast, this long only once the previous winter at the farm down on the Piedra.

The following day the storm raged on, this time with powerful gusts of wind that blew the snow from the trees. Cloyd stayed put. He had the snowshoes but it would be crazy to travel in this storm. He was sure that he'd shaken the men behind him. Even if he hadn't, the snow had come along to cover his tracks.

After two days, the storm had mostly cleared. Squalls were still dropping heavy snow here and there, but the sun was beginning to shine through now and again.

In the openings among the trees, four feet of snow covered the ground.

It was bitterly cold in the wake of the storm. Moving would warm him up. He was wearing all his layers, from his thermal underwear to his bright-red mountaineering shell, and still he was cold. It was time to be moving again. He started out on the snowshoes.

The cubs followed in the trail that Cloyd broke as he headed in the direction of the Ute Creeks. This was an altogether different world from the mountains he'd known two days before. Everything was softer, rounder, quieter. With the white of the snow and the dark green of the spruce timber, the world had only two colors now.

To his surprise, the cubs started looking back, as if they were being followed. They kept looking back, when there was nothing to be seen back there. They yawned with anxiety as Cloyd had seen dogs yawn.

Cloyd trusted the cubs' senses. He shoed faster. If those men were back there, they were using his packed trail, while he had to break the snow.

He was about five hundred feet below the timberline on the steep north slopes of the Pyramid. He came out of the trees now and stood at the opening of a break in the timber two hundred feet across. It was starting to snow heavily again.

Now Cloyd could hear voices behind him. Apparently they didn't know how close he was, or they wouldn't be making any noise. With the muffling effect of this snow, they might be only a minute or two behind him.

Cloyd knew he was looking at an avalanche chute, and he knew that he would try to cross it. There wasn't time to sit down and think. He only knew that he wasn't going to let Rusty catch him.

He held his breath and started out, the bears close on his heels and constantly looking back.

"Don't look down," he was telling himself. He'd caught a glimpse of the dizzying lengths of the chute below, like an endless ski run.

He was almost across. He'd almost made it across when he heard the shouts behind him. With a glance over his shoulder he saw the bright colors of their clothes; that was all. Rusty's gravelly voice was shouting, "Get off of there, Cloyd!"

All Cloyd knew was that he had only twenty yards to go to reach safety. Those men weren't likely to take the chance he had and follow him.

Maybe it was the shouts that set it off, or simply his weight on that particular spot that hair-triggered the snow.

He heard an ominous cracking sound spreading like a chain reaction through the snowpack, and then suddenly he was falling, tumbling and sliding and falling, and he was moving fast, hurtling down the mountain inside the weight of the snow. For a moment he wondered about the bears at his heels and realized that they must be inside the slide too.

The snowshoes had been ripped away immediately, but he was all encumbered by his heavy pack. He felt it dragging him down and killing him. Strangely, a few seconds later he felt weightless. The sensation didn't last long. Abruptly, his body took a terrible pounding on a big bump that crushed the air out of his lungs. At least he was free of the pack—it had been torn off his back. All the time he was hurtling down, down.

He'd thought about avalanches. He'd thought about what they must look like, those monumental waves of snow racing down chutes like the ones in Snowslide Canyon around the mine. In his Living in the Southwest class, his teacher had taken them up onto Coal Bank Pass and taught them about avalanche safety and how to build snow caves.

But he wasn't remembering all these things. Only a trace of what he had learned came to him now, and he didn't know where it was coming from. *Swim,* was all he remembered. Swim toward the surface.

He was swimming, breaststroking as best he could. Swimming toward what he thought was the light. It was hard to tell which way was up and which way was down.

The avalanche was slowing. He realized he was going to stop sliding, and then he remembered at the last moment to bring his hands in front of his face to make an air pocket.

Then all was still. He knew he hadn't ended up on the surface. It felt like he was encased in concrete. He was breathing, he knew that, and he was spitting out the snow that had been imbedded in his mouth. He was buried alive.

So this was the way he would die, he realized. Before long, he would suffocate. He had only a tiny air pocket. How long? Five, ten minutes?

Time was going by, too much time. It was getting harder and harder to breathe. He was beginning to suffocate.

Cloyd never thought of the men far above him beginning to work their way down the edge of the slide. They never came to mind. Only three people came to mind: his grandmother, his sister, and Walter Landis. And the bears came to mind; he'd let them down too.

In case they were nearby, dying somewhere close enough to hear, he would try to talk to them. To let them know he cared about them. He couldn't really talk. Talking would use too much air, and he didn't have the strength. But he could hum. He could make a sound like humming.

Cloyd heard nothing but his own humming until he heard the bears. Their claws were scratching on the hard-packed slide ice above. "Brownie!" he grunted. "Cocoa!"

At last he could see them through ice and snow and claws. He was lying face up, and he could see the faces of his bears come for him, and he could see the sky.

The three men never saw what happened. They were more than a thousand feet above and back in the trees. They didn't see two grizzly cubs swim their way out of the snowslide as it came to rest. They didn't see the cubs walking back and forth over the slide, with their noses down low and their ears up straight. The men didn't see them stop suddenly and cock their ears this way and that. The men didn't see the bear cubs begin to dig furiously at a certain spot. They didn't find out that Cloyd's grave had been only two feet deep.

And the three men didn't see Cloyd rise from the compacted snow. They didn't see him collect the one snowshoe that was sticking out of the slide. They didn't see him disappear with the cubs into the trees on the far side of the slide as he heard the second and larger avalanche from the peak itself come rumbling down the chute. When the men came to the bottom of the slidepath twenty minutes later, all trace of Cloyd and the cubs had been erased.

The dump zone was a hundred yards across and twice as long. The men walked it, looking for signs of the Ute boy or the cubs. They found none. For several hours they probed with branches, then gave Cloyd up for dead. In the spring, they said, it would be safe to return to this place and reclaim the body.

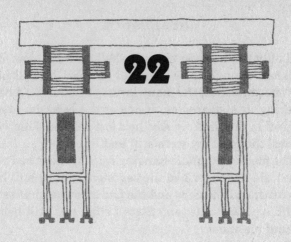

22

Cloyd could manage to shuffle along on one snowshoe if he put almost no weight on the other foot. Often the unsupported leg would sink into the fresh snow and pull him down. He was bruised and freezing, but he was alive. He kept up a stream of talk with the bears, marveling and raving over what they had done.

All Cloyd could think of was Sixto's tent on Middle Ute Creek, the matches and all the supplies in that tent, the big food bag hanging in the tree. Sixto's canvas wall tent wasn't so far away. He could keep shuffling along. He could make it to Middle Ute Creek.

These bears at his side—it was true, they truly were his relatives. They felt it just as much as he felt it.

And they were still alive, still free.

He'd lost the backpack and a snowshoe, and his wool cap that he'd been able to pull down over his ears. He had only the hood on his rain shell for a hat now. But he knew enough to be thankful for what he still had: the one snowshoe, the many layers of clothes he'd been wearing, the snowboots. If one of the boots had been torn off in the slide . . . And he'd lost neither of his wool gloves, though they were stiff and frozen.

The medicine bundle hanging from his neck had survived. He no longer had the bearstone, but he still had the tooth and the claw and the Ute arrowhead. He still had his pocketknife, and Sixto's sling was still belted around his waist.

That was all.

It was a strange feeling, knowing that for all the world he was dead now. Walter would hear that he was dead, his grandmother and his sister would hear that he was dead. Yet his heart was pounding in his chest, strong with the will to live.

As it was getting dark, Cloyd kicked out a well in the snow down to ground level, and then he cut enough spruce branches to make a bed six inches thick. The worst cold always seemed to come right up through the ground. His shelter had no roof, but the snow walls cut the wind. There was nothing to do but lie down and pull the bears close against him. He maneuvered his arms back through the sleeves of his thermal underwear, his flannel shirt, his sweatshirt, his pile jacket, and his rain shell. He had to keep his hands close against his body, or his fingers would freeze.

The bears huddled close. Exhausted, he fell asleep with one bear against his belly and chest, and the other wrapped around his head.

*   *   *

Cloyd came off the mountain at the place where East and Middle Ute Creeks flowed together, and he turned up the middle branch. The cubs were gnawing the willows along the stream, finding the bark to their liking. Cloyd carried the one snowshoe under his arm as he followed the line of trees along the edge of the meadow. There was little snow under the trees, and only a foot and a half had fallen on the meadow. Not nearly so much had fallen down on the Ute Creeks as above on the slopes of the Pyramid.

Sixto's tent would be waiting for him only a few miles up the meadow. His spirits were soaring. The bears were finding the white world to their liking. They were striking the snow with their forepaws, rolling in it, biting it, chasing their shadows. As Cloyd walked the edge of the trees, Brownie and Cocoa stayed out in the meadow, clawing here and there through the snow for grass and roots.

At first glance Cloyd couldn't tell what was wrong. But magpies meant mischief, and he could hear magpies squawking up there around the campsite. Usually they congregated around a carcass. Cloyd was squinting into the bright sunlight bouncing off the snow, and he could see just enough to know something was wrong with the tent. He started to run. The tent was all out of shape, barely standing. The storm?

Once Cloyd saw the gashes in the canvas, he stopped running. As he walked up on the scene, his eyes took in the devastation. Everything was ripped and strewn and destroyed. The canned goods had been set up along a log and then exploded with shots from a high-powered rifle. Brownie and Cocoa were lapping at the remains of their contents. "No!" he shouted, and lunged at them, striking one and bowling the other over. "Get out of there!" he raged. "Leave this garbage alone! You have to be wild! You get around garbage, there'll be people there! Some of them will be afraid of you! They'll kill you!"

The cubs kept away and watched, all abashed and intimidated, as he picked up the shredded remains of a can of stew. The cubs had never seen him all mad like this. Good, he thought.

Cloyd snatched up an empty feed sack and began picking up the mess. When he was done he tossed the sack into the branches of a tree, and then he turned to the mutilated tent. Only one pole was holding it up. Even the guy lines to the pegs had been cut. All around the campsite there were pieces of destruction, some showing and others hidden under the snow.

He went around picking things up, turning the objects over in his hands, mourning for everything that had been lost. He was sorry for himself, but he felt even worse for Sixto. The old sheepherder had left him his whole camp, all his valuable possessions. What would he ever say to Sixto, how would he make up for it?

Who would do this? Why? Why would anyone do this?

Then his eye fell on something these people had brought and left here—a big, empty whiskey bottle. Now he could see what had happened. Whoever it was, they'd gotten drunk and done all this for no reason at all, only to amuse themselves with their own meanness.

The sheepherder stove had been broken into pieces,

the chimney had been flattened, the food bag had been
cut down out of the tree and all its contents slashed
and scattered. The flashlight Sixto had retrieved from
the entrance of the mine had been smashed. Inside the
tent, Cloyd found the pots and pans crushed, the blankets tossed around. Where was the box of big kitchen
matches? Seven matches, soaked under the snow that
had fallen in through the wide gashes in the canvas,
were all he could find.

Seven matches.

He wanted to get away from this place, to lead the
cubs away as quickly as he could. But first he had to
collect everything that might be useful: the matches,
a skillet, one dented cooking pot, a big spoon, the remains of the bag of flour, a little lard, a can of peaches
and one of apricots that the marksmen had missed, the
beans the magpies hadn't already carried away, all the
parachute cord and rope he could salvage, pieces of
canvas, the two blankets that hadn't been damaged at
all, and the small folding army shovel the vandals had
also overlooked. With a strip from one of the blankets,
he could make a headband to save his ears from the
cold. He bundled all this salvage into the largest piece
of canvas, and he slung it over his shoulder and walked
off.

The snow on the meadows was melting. Not fast, but
it was melting. The sun was out, and his wool gloves
were drying. He was angry, and he was hurt, but he
felt himself lifting with determination. He wasn't going
to let this drive him out of the mountains.

Cloyd made his camp where he had camped with the
old man, at the second site along East Ute Creek. He

173

made a low-ceilinged lean-to of cut branches for a shelter. He retrieved the bearskin from the tree where he had cached it, and used it for a third blanket at night. Storms could blow through the Window high above and around the Pyramid. He resolved to carry through what he had started. Now he wanted to see the cubs safely into winter.

The problem was denning. The grizzly woman and the game warden who had cared about bears had agreed that denning was the problem. The cubs might not dig a den from instinct. If they did, they might only scratch out an approximation of one, which wouldn't take them through the winter. They would freeze to death in a den that wasn't good enough.

Maybe how to dig the den was something they would have learned from their mother.

He could dig the den for them. He had the folding camp shovel. But he knew they wouldn't den for a while yet. If he could find any food to add to the meager supplies he'd brought from the ruins of Sixto's camp, he could stay with them awhile. There were snowshoe hares around; he'd seen one or two, almost completely turned white. Every day he practiced long hours with the sling, with smooth round rocks he fished out of the creek.

Cloyd was putting off using the seven matches. The sun had dried them out and they looked serviceable, but he had to save them. He ate the can of apricots first, and then, after a few days, the can of peaches. He savored each bite, and he drank the juice slowly. Hunger was gnawing at him, but it was a pain he could tolerate if he kept his mind off it. He was good at doing without things; that was something that went way back with him.

There was another idea in the back of his mind. He realized this idea had been planted when he'd first found the arrowhead. All the deer and all the elk hadn't dropped to lower elevations when the snowstorm had come. There was a big bull elk he was seeing every day on the meadow, digging up the grass. If he could make an arrow for his arrowhead, and a bow for the arrow, and if he could sneak up extremely close . . .

It took three of his matches to start a fire. He was hungry, and he cooked up a few *gordas*. He had half a dozen arrows ready that he'd fashioned from dead willow. He hardened the points of five in the fire. It might be possible to take small game without an arrowhead.

It was easy to come by the feathers. With bits of his *gordas* he lured the gray jays in close, then baited the spot under the deadfall trap he'd constructed. A tug on a piece of cord, and the log would sometimes drop on the bird. Brownie and Cocoa watched his technique with admiration. The cubs could eat as many jays as he could provide.

His bow, when he was done with it, looked barely sturdy enough. It might work if he was lucky. Parachute cord would have to do for a bowstring. With thread he'd taken from the seams in the canvas, he tied the feathers to the arrow shaft and hafted the arrowhead to the arrow.

The days of mid-October Cloyd spent hunting, mostly for that solitary bull elk that was still too stubborn to abandon the high country. Cloyd stalked it in the twilight, in the cold, gray hours on either side of the ever-shortening days. Despite his gloves and snowboots, his fingers and toes always ached with cold. During the day he would lie shivering in wait beside the elk trails, waiting for his prey to walk by at close range.

He'd heard stories of animals that would offer themselves to the hunter, simply show themselves up close and allow the hunter to take their lives as a gift. The big bull elk knew Cloyd was hunting him, but this elk hadn't grown so old by being generous. Cloyd could remember times when deer had walked right into his and Walter's camp on this very meadow. One morning while they were eating breakfast, three spike bucks had walked into camp, big-eyed, curious, to within fifteen feet of them as Cloyd and Walter stood there sipping cocoa and just watching.

But those curious young deer were gone. There was only this one enormous, cautious elk with antlers three feet high and just as wide.

When he wasn't hunting the elk, Cloyd was practicing with the sling. There was a scree slope that came down to the meadow on the other side of the creek, and there was a big marmot who taunted him from those rocks. He'd let many a stone fly at that whistle pig, and he'd come within a whisker several times.

The days were coming so clear, bright, and blue, one after the next, that it was an afterthought when he realized he needed to make another snowshoe. Winter could come back at any time. He knew he wasn't thinking well. He should have made the snowshoe even before the bow and arrow.

For two days he worked on the showshoe, until he knew it was strong enough. He fashioned the frame from green willow branches, and he wove canvas strips and smaller branches to make the webbing. Canvas strips served for the binding to hold his boot.

All the time he was keeping track of the days, marking them on a stick with his knife. The day of the slide had been the eleventh of October. Ten days had passed since then. The days were growing ominously short, and his hunger was hurting him all the time. He used two more matches to start a fire to make his last pot of beans, his last *gordas*.

It had to be time, he thought, for making the den. The beans and *gordas* gave him the strength he needed. He took the cubs and ranged the mountainside up above the meadow, up in the spruce trees. Between the meadow and the barren heights above the tree line, a dense forest of spruce swathed the steep slopes at the foot of the Continental Divide. It was the kind of site Sixto had described, a north-facing slope that would lie in the shadows all winter, out of the path of the sun. All winter long the Divide's towering ridge, which included the Window, would block the sun. In the shadows, the snows would accumulate deep and undisturbed to shelter the den over the entire span of deep winter.

At last Cloyd found a place he liked, a steep bank under a massive spruce, whose roots would hold the ceiling and keep it from collapsing.

The ground was frozen and made for hard digging at first. It was slow work with the tiny shovel. But it was a good tool and sturdy. He could use it as a shovel or adjust the blade at right angles and use it as a pick.

The cubs showed little interest until the morning of the second day, when he broke through into unfrozen dirt. They began digging beside him. He kept the entrance small, only big enough for him to crawl through.

Cloyd tunneled back eight feet before he started making the sleeping chamber. As he chipped out dirt and rock and pushed it behind him, the cubs pushed it out the rest of the way. All the while he talked to them. "This is where you're going to make your big sleep. Any day now. You go in here and fall asleep real soon, Cocoa. You got that, Brownie?"

Without food he couldn't work, and so he used up the last of it and the last of his matches.

Late the third day the work was done. The den extended fourteen feet into the mountain. Strong roots in the ceiling convinced Cloyd he'd made a den that couldn't collapse on the cubs. The sleeping chamber was round, six feet across and four feet high.

Every day after that, he visited the den. He would go inside the den each day with the bears, bringing soft branches with him, hoping they would lie down on the branches and go to sleep for the winter. They joined him in lining the den with more spruce boughs, but they showed no interest in staying inside the den. They would soon go outside to play on the slope, while he would try to call them back into the den.

Somehow they knew. For some reason, the time wasn't right.

Or else they didn't have the idea at all.

He was so hungry, he'd often stumble from light-headedness. But he was so close now, he couldn't turn and leave. Any day now, the cubs should den up.

The day came when he had his chance at the solitary elk. He was kneeling behind a bush when the elk appeared in the little clearing along one of the paths it had been using. Cloyd had been daydreaming that he was standing in a hot shower and letting the steaming water pour over and over him. Suddenly he saw, like an apparition, the immense antlers, the great head, the dark ruff around the neck. With a few more steps, the elk was standing in full view, not twenty feet away. Then the bull began to dig in the snow with a front hoof. Cloyd bent the bow back, trying to get enough force behind this one piece of stone to find the animal's heart. . . .

Before he was quite ready, the bow made a cracking sound. He let the arrow fly anyway. The elk was gone.

At once he realized that he had forgotten to thank the animal for its life. Even when he slaughtered goats and sheep, he had always done that.

Cloyd didn't see the elk after that. In the night it snowed again, and even the last stubborn solitary bull elk in the high country knew it was time to leave.

It wasn't a big snow, only six inches. But four or five days in a row, these snows came. When he could venture out, he gnawed on willow bark alongside the bears, and once they led him to a thicket of serviceberries where the berries had dried in place rather than dropped to the ground.

It turned much colder, and the wind blew until he thought the spruces might break. This cold was worse than any he had known before. He was wearing the bearskin again. He laced it tight with parachute cord around his limbs and up his belly and chest. The cold still found his bones, but it couldn't kill him. Every day he led the cubs to the den, and went into the den with them and begged them to stay.

Their stomachs were shrinking, he knew. The grizzly woman had said that for a week or so before hibernation, they ate almost nothing and didn't need food.

But he did. He was starving. His body had turned on him some time before and had been eating its own fat and then his muscles. He had his chance at a snowshoe hare with the sling, but it was white against the snow, and his stone barely missed. "Sleep, bears," he pleaded, "while I still have a chance to go home."

23

It was November now, Cloyd guessed, but he'd forgotten some time before to make the notches in the stick and so he'd lost track. The temperatures were dropping below zero, how far below he couldn't guess. The creek was iced over except for pockets here and there. As he walked about, the snow crunched loudly under his boots. The nights were so much longer than the days. He slept in the den with the cubs now. He should have thought of it sooner, but he hadn't been thinking well. It was so much warmer inside the earth and out of the wind. The air in the confines of the den was warmed by the breathing of the bears, and his own breath. Inside the earth, with his clothes and the bearskin and the two blankets, he wasn't cold.

The nights were long. Cloyd's sleep was starved and restless. He'd lie awake remembering White Mesa, the

aromatic sagebrush, the smell of juniper wood burning.
He'd drift into sleep seeing the shapes of the mesas
and the slickrock rims of the hidden canyons. Above
the mesas and the canyons, Blue Mountain would be
riding on a cloud. He could hear his grandmother's and
his sister's voices, like music. They were gathering
piñon nuts. He was calling to them, but they couldn't
hear him. He could hear a raven thrashing by, but he
couldn't see it. The moon was rising over a sheer red
wall. A goat was blatting, and water was trickling over
a pour-off.

Twice in the den, he dreamed of the farm. The first
time, it was raining and raining and would never quit.
The cottonwood trees, bare except for a few golden
leaves, were collapsing into the raging river. The old
man was standing there, watching the river eat away
at the headgate, where the big valve in the concrete
gate let the water into his ditch. Every minute huge
chunks of dark earth were tearing loose and collapsing
into the river. "There's nothing we can do!" the old man
cried, and he threw up his hands. Then the river broke
through and it went tearing down the pasture in a
surging flood. The house and the barn were immediately stranded on an island, with the river raging by
around both sides. Before he woke, Cloyd saw the water
all gone, but so was the big barn, and there was nothing
but boulders where there used to be hayfields and pastures and an orchard.

The second time he dreamed of the farm, he'd just
gotten off the bus from school where it dropped him on
the highway. He walked that mile to the farm all night
in his dreams, knowing somehow that he would find

the old man dead inside the house when he eventually got there.

It wasn't only in the den that Cloyd dreamed. He dreamed in the daytime too, in the sunshine or in the shadows or with the snow falling on his hair. There was nothing to do now but wait, wait for the cubs to den or for his own body to eat itself up from the inside.

There hadn't been one certain day that had come along when he'd made this decision to stay until the end. It was all the days passing, one day after the other, as he'd grown accustomed to his hunger and accepted it. He knew now that he would die here. He would never have the strength to leave. It was a strange fate for him, that he would choose this death, that he would die for these two bears. Yet it was a death that belonged to him, and he could accept it.

Next summer the grizzly woman would return, and she would find these bears alive.

Every day now, Cloyd stood in place for long periods of time, doing the steps of the bear dance in place. Barely moving his feet, he danced the three steps forward, three steps back. He was dancing himself into the dream that had started when he'd found the bearstone, maybe even before that, when he was little and first heard the thunder coming off the big resonating drum, the scratching and growling of bears.

As he danced himself into a trance every day, his traveling soul would leave his body, as it had left his body the time he had risen above the Bear Dance and seen the dancing from above. His traveling soul soared above East Ute Creek, and he could see three bear forms down there—two cubs and the grizzly with a

183

human face standing upright, barely shuffling its feet, three steps forward, three steps back.

His traveling soul lifted up, up, until it was soaring over the Divide, above the Window, above the Rio Grande Pyramid. All the world was cloaked with snow, all the thousand peaks were softened and all the valleys softened, and it was a world more silent and restful than any he had ever known.

When the light turned down every day, he led the cubs back up the steep slope to the den.

He began making notches in the stick again, but his mind no longer turned the notches into meaning. He no longer differentiated between the dreams of his denning sleep and his waking dreams on the meadow. It was all a dream that he was living inside of now, a dream not far from death.

Yet his body was stubborn and had reserves greater than he would have known. He was still standing, still doing the bear dance.

His traveling soul was out of his body and up on the Divide. The sun was high in the sky; the berries were ripe; he was eating sweet berries in a thicket high on the Divide. With no warning came a terrible roar, and he fell back onto the ground. An enormous bear with brown fur tipped with silver was standing over him, and it had an arrow in its neck and one in its chest. Blood was streaming from the bear's wounds and from its mouth, and it was shaking its head back and forth and roaring horribly.

"What do you want with me?" he said to the bear.

"Who are you?" the bear roared.

"I'm a Weminuche Ute," he answered. He knew that he owed this bear for something and that his time had come to give back. "I know why you have come," he told the bear. "I give you permission now."

He watched from outside as the great bear tore the flesh from his bones and left them scattered and gleaming on the ground.

Now the bear reappeared with no arrows and no blood streaming from his wounds.

He didn't know where the song came from, but he knew there was a song he was supposed to sing to this bear, and he knew the words to the song. He sang,

> *"Whu! Bear!*
> *Whu Whu!*
> *So you say*
> *Whu Whu Whu!*
> *You come.*
> *You're a fine young man*
> *You Grizzly Bear*
> *You crawl out of your fur.*
> *You come*
> *I say Whu Whu Whu!*
> *I throw grease in the fire.*
> *For you*
> *Grizzly Bear*
> *We are the same person!"*

The bear was pleased with his song. "Here, I will help you," the bear said, and together they began reassembling his bones. When his skeleton was fully reassembled, the bear touched each of his bones and called them by name, and new flesh grew on his bones.

He was himself again.

Now the bear had the head of a bear and the body of a human being. "Who are you?" Cloyd asked.

"I'm the keeper of the animals," the bear-man replied. "Listen carefully. There is one animal, white as the snow, that stays among the peaks even in winter. Take your best weapon and climb high until you find this animal. You have my permission to take him to sustain your own life."

When Cloyd's feet came to rest, he remembered every detail of his dream.

The following morning he shed the bearskin and told the cubs to stay behind. They watched him go. He could still see them down there on the snowbound meadow, far below, when he had cleared the tree line and was inching toward the Divide.

He wasn't wearing the snowshoes. These slopes had already shed their snow once, and the snow didn't lie deep enough as yet to slide again. He couldn't climb but two or three steps at a time before he ran out of air and out of strength. He barely had the strength to lift his legs, but he kept climbing.

With a glance over his shoulder he noticed his tracks, and, it was curious to note, he was leaving the tracks of a bear.

He was living inside the spirit world now.

After a time the Window came into view high above him. Toward the Window he climbed, the center point of his spirit world. Vaguely he knew he'd been there before, that it was important to him, this towering gap in the sky. He'd been there more than once. But he couldn't remember when or how, or what had happened there.

And so the Window drew him on and up. When he'd

nearly reached it, and the towering rockwalls on either side seemed to take up all the world except the gap of sky between them, he sat down and looked back the way he'd come. There were peaks strung all along the horizon, jagged snowbound peaks that seemed familiar, but he couldn't remember their names. He wondered why he had come here. He wondered what he was doing on the top of the world, when it was all cloaked in winter.

He sat there a long time. He couldn't think of a reason to go up or to go down. After a time something odd caught his eyes, something on the slope not so far away. Two strips of black in the snow, curling away from each other. Raven feathers? Now they were moving as if they were alive, and moving in unison. He blinked and looked closer. An animal was moving toward him from across the slope.

A mountain goat, he realized. The "feathers" were the black horns of a mountain goat. Then he remembered who he was and why he had climbed this mountain. Slowly, he took the sling from his waist and fitted a stone to it, keeping another ready in his left hand.

The white goat kept coming on, along the trace of a goat path, walking right toward him. Now he could see that there were two more goats following at some distance.

The leader was a yearling, filled with curiosity. Its winter coat had grown out long and shaggy, and all Cloyd could see to aim at were the horns and the eyes and the nose.

When the goat was thirty feet away from him, it stopped and stood still, nibbled the lichens on a rock, then turned its head sideways as if to give him a better target. Cloyd thanked the goat as he had thanked the many goats he had slaughtered when he was growing up with his grandmother, and then he whirled the sling.

The stone sank into the soft spot behind the goat's eye. The goat stood for a second, and then all four legs collapsed. Cloyd went to it and bled the goat with his knife. The animal's quivering ceased.

The liver was warm, and he chewed it slowly. At first it came back up, but then his stomach began to accept it.

Slowly, slowly, he carried the goat down the mountain on his shoulder, dragging it when he fell under its weight. As soon as he got down, he would skin it. He could make a hat out of that shaggy fur, a hat big enough to pull down over his ears.

The cubs were not as interested in food as he had thought they would be. They ate the heart and a few scraps of fat, but that was all.

When he denned with the cubs that night, he didn't dream. He was filled with purpose. All he could think about were the components of the bow drill. He'd come very close to making fire on the blacktop behind the school that next-to-last day of the school year. He'd made plenty of smoke, almost fire.

The next day he worked all day long at making a bow drill. The bow itself was only a third of the size of his failed hunting bow. Parachute cord was fine for the string, his teacher had said. His best arrow, cut short, would make a good drill. One end of the drill would turn in the brace he was carving for his palm. The other, sharper end would turn in the tiny socket he dug out in the soft board he'd shaped from a dry piece of spruce.

He worked hard on his tinder, shredding bark and mixing it with needles and the finest of twigs.

The hard part had always been transferring his coals from the board to his tinder. That's when his coals had always gone out.

Seven times, the same thing happened. He'd worked all afternoon making tinder and working the bow. The daylight was going, and he was all out of hope.

"I don't mind failing," the old man had said, "as long as I tried my best."

Haven't I tried my best? Cloyd thought. What else can I do?

Just then, he had an idea of his own. It was a simple idea, maybe a good one.

This time he dug a little depression in the ground, and he placed his nest of tinder in the depression. When his kindling was ready, he began to work the bow back and forth, faster and faster, as the cubs sat attentively and watched.

He was making plenty of smoke, and the fine coals that were being produced in the soft spruce were falling out of the socket and into the nest of tinder. He kept making that bow sing. More and more coals were falling into the nest, without the need of being transferred from the board, and the tinder itself was smoking.

When the moment was right, he blew on the nest of tinder.

And it exploded into flame. He could see in the cubs' eyes, they thought he'd made magic.

He went to sleep with a warm belly. He'd made plenty

of coals and then smothered them so they would burn slowly all night. But even if they weren't still alive in the morning, he could make fire again with the bow drill as the old Utes had.

The next four days, the cubs wouldn't eat any meat at all. They went in and out of the den, sniffing the wind, pacing. Cloyd could tell a big storm was coming in. Maybe this storm was what the cubs were waiting for.

The snow started to fall in the evening and fell hard all night. This was powder snow, the kind he remembered from midwinter at the farm. It fell for three days, and the cubs watched one evening from the tunnel as it covered up all their tracks into the den.

Apparently they were satisfied. No enemies would track them to their den. When they went to sleep that night, Cloyd heard their hearts slow down, beating more slowly than he had ever heard before. Their breath came much less often. In the morning, their hearts were beating even slower. He said good-bye to them, each one aloud by name. They didn't stir. He knew he could leave them now.

"Good-bye, Cocoa," he said again. "Good-bye, Brownie."

He squeezed quietly through the tunnel toward the soft light, and they didn't follow. Before he started down the slope, he watched a long time. The snow was beginning to pile up around the entrance, and it was quickly covering his tracks.

This was the big storm that was the proof of winter, the storm the bears had been waiting for. There'd be no melting here on these shadowy slopes until spring.

He knew what he had to do. He would cook up all the goat meat he could carry, he would fashion a pack out of canvas and rope, and he would start over the Divide. At its shortest, the route down the Pine River was twenty-five miles long. But he would travel far out of his way to avoid the avalanche chutes.

He waited three days after the storm. He could hear the snow sliding off the peaks, and he could wait until it had settled down.

Then he started out. If anyone had seen him, they would have thought they'd seen a snowshoeing grizzly.

But no one was in the backcountry, no one at all. No one marked his slow and painful progress, in a week's time, over the Divide and down the valley of the Pine.

No one saw him until he walked through the door of the Cowboy Bar, four miles beyond the Pine River trailhead, at the end of the plowed road around the northern tip of Vallecito Reservoir. The men and the women there didn't see the bearskin when he came to the door; it was rolled up in his pack with the blankets. They saw a dark-skinned Ute boy with long, shaggy black hair under a strange peaked cap of white fur that was streaked with blood. His lips were blackened, cracked, and bleeding. He was wearing a red mountaineering shell, top and trousers, smeared with dried blood. They could see that he was unused to speaking. They could see that he'd suffered much. None of the men and women there was saying a word; they only stared. He said, "Would somebody drive me to Walter Landis's place on the Piedra River?"

*   *   *

He asked the man to drop him at the highway. He didn't want to drive in. He'd come all this way, he could walk a mile more.

It was just turning dark when he reached the orchard and caught sight of the old farmhouse in the spruce trees. There was no smoke coming out of the chimney, and he was filled with dread. Walter Landis was dead, his heart was telling him. Walter is dead, I've come too late.

He went into the mudroom without knocking, and he didn't take off any of his clothes or his boots. He opened the next door and stood between the kitchen and the parlor. The house was cold. No lights were on.

He switched on the parlor light, and a figure stirred there in the far corner, in the easy chair. The old man was blinking to try to adjust to the light, and he was trying to understand who it was he was seeing there at the entrance of the parlor.

"It's me," Cloyd said. "It's me."

The old man looked, and looked again, and wiped his hands over his eyes, and stared.

"It's really me," Cloyd said, and then he walked over to the old man and put a hand on his shoulder.

"Lord, lord," the old man said, still uncertain. "Rusty said you were dead."

"It's cold in here," Cloyd said disapprovingly. "You forgot to make a fire."

Ashen-faced, Walter was struggling to his feet. "You're alive," he said. "You're not dead." The old man reached with both hands and placed them on Cloyd's shoulders. He was looking Cloyd up and down in wonder. "I'll bet you've got a story to tell. . . . You look like something the cat spit out."

Cloyd took his medicine bundle from around his neck and brought out the coin for Walter. It was hard to work the fingers on his right hand. The index finger was numb and useless from frostbite. But he brought out the coin for Walter between his thumb and his middle finger.

The old man reached for his reading glasses on the end table and put them on. "Spanish gold piece," he marveled. "Where'd you find it?"

"In the mountains," Cloyd said with a grin. It was as specific as he was ever going to get.

The old man was coming to life now. He grinned back. His skin was glowing red instead of pale white. "We've got to get a fire started . . . I nodded off . . . I was going to when I woke up. Say, have I got something for you. . . ." The old man disappeared into his room, then quickly returned with a huge smile on his face and a small turquoise carving of a bear held out on his palm. "Guess what Rusty found smack in a fresh bear scat back in the mountains."

Cloyd took it between his thumb and middle finger. Yes, it really was the bearstone.

"They can't take those cubs out of the mountains now," Cloyd said.

"No, they won't, and Rusty'll be awful happy to hear they're alive. It was you he was after rather than those bears. . . . I sent him, Cloyd. I knew if anyone could find you, he could. Rusty was going to help bring you out and let you know they decided to leave those bears alone."

"Good," Cloyd said. He was so weary. "That's good," he said.

"Let me tell you a secret that will never go beyond the three of us. You know how Rusty's always been one to take the law into his own hands. . . . You'll never guess what he brought back from Alaska and let go in the Weminuche Wilderness in September: a yearling grizzly! Caught it in a culvert trap and drove it back to Colorado. He said it had to be a male, to make up for the one he killed. He was hoping at least one of yours turned out to be a female."

Cloyd closed his fingers on the bearstone. "They both are."

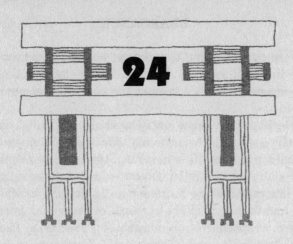

24

The sun was climbing higher in the sky, and each day it cleared the Divide for a few more minutes. Each day the sun shone a few minutes longer on the steep slope below the Window and above East Ute Creek. All winter long, this slope had lain in the shadows in the grip of extreme cold. But the sun had arrived, and winter was giving way to spring even at 11,600 feet on the shady side of the Divide.

At 7,000 feet, on a farm at the edge of the wilderness, a Ute boy was doing the bear dance, even though it was early March and the Bear Dance wouldn't be held until nearly the end of May. It was a tradition he had learned, that the people helped the bears to awaken after their long sleep.

He had selected a special place to perform his bear dance. He'd climbed high above the farm to the place where he had found the ancient blue stone carved in the image of a grizzly. He'd walked the ledge and now stood on the chalky floor of the cave high above the farm.

He hoped to dance until he could see things that otherwise would be invisible. For a gift, he knew he should give something in return. He'd shinnied behind the slab that had fallen from the roof of the cave, and he had replaced the bearstone in the pottery jar where he had found it. To the remains of the infant buried there, wrapped in a robe of rabbit fur and turkey feathers, he'd whispered "Thank you." He didn't need to carry the bearstone any longer. The strength of the bear was inside him.

As he faced the snow-clad tips of the mountains showing above the canyon of the Piedra, his dancing deepened, until it carried him above the forests and even above the Divide. He could see all over. On the slopes facing the sun, the first flowers were blooming and the first patches of grass greening. Water was trickling at the edges of the snowbanks, rivulets were rushing from underneath them, and marmots were whistling from the rockslides.

He saw the place he was looking for, a small hole in the snow beneath an immense spruce tree, on a slope he well remembered. There was a bit of water dripping from an icicle suspended above the hole.

A sharp nose was poking its way out, and now a broad face, bright and curious, was looking out on the world all shining and new. A second face appeared, and two bears, one brown and one the shade of cocoa, pushed through the snow and sat in front of their den, sniffing the spring wind and the scent of growing things newly come to life.

He had found his dream.

He saw them tumble and slide down the slope with their old playfulness, and he saw them lope across the crusted white meadow in that shuffling gait of the grizzly, with their heads carried close to the ground.

They were going to grow wild and large and powerful, and go about their ancient ways. If he ever came across them again, they might stand and pause and wonder. But then they would turn and go. They had known him in a bear's dream, and he had known them in his.

Author's Note

Although *Beardance* is fiction, all of the places in the story are real places I know from more than thirty backpacking trips. Lake Mary Alice, for example, is one of my favorite destinations. The first time I visited Mary Alice, at the foot of Mount Oso, I witnessed the colossal water, ice, and rockfall described in *Beardance*.

I believe there's a part of the human heart that longs for wild places. That part of my heart is filled with the forests, alpine tundra, and snow-clad peaks of the Weminuche Wilderness in the San Juan Mountains of southwestern Colorado.

Years before I ever thought of writing *Beardance*, I was gathering the knowledge and experiences that would lead me to this story. In 1973, soon after my wife and I came to live in southwestern Colorado, we found teaching jobs in the little town of Pagosa Springs. I was lucky enough to be able to start a class called Living in the Southwest. Along with my students I was interviewing local old-timers, exploring in the library, and learning about the human history and natural history of the San Juans. We learned about the legend of the Lost Mine of the Window and the ways of the old sheepherders, and we learned about our neighbors the Utes who still dance the Bear Dance every spring to help bring the bears out of hibernation.

We learned that grizzlies had been plentiful here during the ten thousand or more years that people lived in the San Juans before the miners and settlers came flooding in during the 1870s. And we learned that now there were no more grizzly bears left in Colorado. The last one had been trapped and killed by a government trapper near the Rio Grande Pyramid in 1952.

What got me started writing *Bearstone*, which came before *Beardance*, was the surprising news in 1979 that a grizzly had been killed in the San Juan Mountains, not far from where we were living. The bear was killed by an outfitter who said he didn't realize it was a grizzly. I began to imagine a story about a Ute boy meeting the last grizzly in Colorado. This being fiction, I got to make up how it would all happen. The boy became Cloyd, with Walter and Rusty soon joining the story.

After that 1979 incident, the experts once again agreed that the grizzlies were all gone. They were extinct in Colorado. I would never have had the heart to invent the idea for *Beardance* if there hadn't been reason to hope that there might still be some left after all. It was a 1990 sighting of a mother grizzly and three cubs by a rancher on horseback that gave me that hope. In the summers following the sighting, bear biologists tested hair samples and other evidence found in the area, and announced that these remote mountains of southwestern Colorado may indeed be home to a few surviving grizzlies.

Now I could begin to imagine Cloyd returning to the mountains and meeting the mate and the cubs of the bear that had been killed in *Bearstone.* After reading for months, learning all I could about grizzlies and the traditions of native people all across the continent regarding bears, I began work on the novel. I found myself struggling with my early chapters, trying to get the story to come to life, so I decided to take a break from my desk and hike back up to the Window, that spectacular notch in the continental divide that I pictured as the geographic focus of the story.

Standing in the Window, I could imagine I saw Cloyd and Walter camping down on East Ute Creek far below. I could almost see the entrance to the lost gold mine on the ridge above the creek. And I could imagine Cloyd with the two grizzly cubs, Brownie and Cocoa, as the snow was beginning to fall. I practically ran home, my head bursting with ideas. I poured all of my love of the mountains and of bears into the writing, as well as my deep respect for native traditions.

I found my fingers flying all day and into the night. In writing, as in reading, you're imagining what it's like to be someone else, and I was fully imagining being Cloyd Atcitty, at 11,800 feet with winter coming on, risking his life for those grizzly cubs. I completed the novel in a sort of trance, much like his, in a little less than a month. It was a wonderful experience, and I don't know if one like it will ever come again.

Will Hobbs